THE DEAL

Matt Cundrick

ACKNOWLEDGEMENTS

To my amazing wife and daughter, who pushed me, and supported me, to fulfil a lifelong ambition in getting here.

To Howard, for friendship and encouragement. As well as the incredible artwork.

To all my friends and family for their advice, critique, and comment. In particular, Tina, Angela, and Chris.

1

The phone buzzed in his pocket. Without losing focus on the conversation, he hit the side buttons a few times.

"I don't agree." he huffed into the room.

The sense of dejection barely noticeable across the walnut table. A slight slump of the shoulders. A tired, frustrated blink, lasted only a split second longer than it should, but noticeable, and this was just how he liked it.

He slowly sipped his pale, tepid coffee.

"These are too low. What are you basing them on?"

The two besuited men opposite ran through their well rehearsed script. It bored him. Frustrated him more.

At this point his face would be spelling it out. He had spent years cultivating his uncompromising approach to these situations, the only problem being, many around the company were sharing notes on how to handle him. Not that it ever worked. It just resulted in more frustration, and more disappointment on their part.

"Look." stopping the younger of the two mid-sentence "go back to trading and have another look at the numbers and send it over later. I've got a 9.30." Clearly they weren't getting anywhere fast.

Thanking him for his time, through gritted teeth, they made their exit. Leaving the office in a rare moment of peace. He stood, mug in hand, and made his way over to the imposing corner desk. Placing his mug on one of the many stained circles left by its predecessors.

He tapped open his iPad screen, for a cursory check of emails. Nothing his half-decent PA couldn't resolve herself. Opening a new message, he flicked uncomfortably over the flimsy keyboard.

Give Mark a shout for me, need to see him first thing tomorrow. Cheers, S

Send. He glanced out of the window.

He could hardly abide small talk in person, let alone in emails. Charlotte, his PA knew this well enough by now. She'd only been in the role 2 months, but was learning fast, especially with his new role. Like those before her in his previous position, she wouldn't last long, but was handling things well while she was around. The Office Diamonds conveyor belt continued to supply him with half-attractive 20-somethings who could handle him for a year or so before his short temper, or short manner, led them to pursue other opportunities.

Steve Bellingham was not an angry man. Like many in his position, he was driven, ruthless, and tough. 'A no nonsense pure-bred operator' the trade press recently described him the day his promotion to Chief Operating Officer was announced. A 'brawler' was the slightly less flattering version. Over a decade in this company had not done wonders for his reputation, so good relationships with the editors were, painfully, necessary. Especially in his new role.

Proving over 20 years working in and around retail, his ability to paint statistical pictures of success always allowed him to shine. Most people didn't like working with him, or for him, but those he worked for, loved him. Ruthlessly unaccepting of poor performance, or those who didn't agree with him, he surrounded himself with those who would, not those who could. Proudly wearing the badge of each dismissal, and each tribunal that followed.

He kept the right people close to him, anyone he thought could add value later in life was in his phone book. This now included senior Directors, Bankers, and even the odd Politician. It was one of these contacts that opened the door at Russell's. They weren't even recruiting at the time, always preferring people who knew the way the company worked, and promoting from within. A former boss from his time at FreshLocal convenience stores was a non-executive Director at the time, and was lobbying the stoic Board of Directors to change their approach.

Eventually, Steve had been asked to meet the Founder, John Russell, at Gordano services on the M5. The far from glamorous location truly fitting with the approach of the business, but Steve knew how to switch on the charm when needed. A distinct ability to be everything the other person didn't even know they needed. Russell was sold in a heartbeat, blinded by the starlight. He had offered him a role there and then, probably the most progressive thing he had done in 20 years. As Steve had left, Russell was giving his HR Director a dressing down in order to create room for him in the company.

Head Of Operational Communications at Russell's Retail had hardly been the glamour role, it did have huge influence over the company, and the salary was OK. However, it was the long term opportunity that really piqued his interest. Like very few at his age, he had an ability to read complex business politics with exceptional accuracy. The company was due change. The ageing CEO, and Founder, combined with a lack of driving force on the board to fill those shoes, would offer him what he craved. It would take a strong shoulder, and firm boots, to get to the front of the queue but this had never been an issue for him.

Less than a month later he had arrived for his first day at their head offices, on a stormy, wet, Tuesday. The building was a classic 1980s block. Something that wouldn't have been out of place in a Russian suburb. A concrete clad, 4 storey monstrosity, hidden away on a windy back road just outside Stevenage. Luckily, some would say. Aluminium framed, single pane windows propped open by box files, despite the rain, gave some indication of the conditions within.

Overgrown cedar trees, and conifers framed the company car park. Full of a mixture of mid-level Fords and Vauxhalls, matching the sky's own palette of grey. He found a quiet corner with lots of empty spaces, and pulled into one. Turning off the engine, he sat back, taking a deep breath. In his head, running through his plan, finely tuned given his career to date. Never one to normally subscribe to a cliched idiom, but in this world, first impressions do count. Every job he had, he made sure he started as he meant to go on, from the first minute to the last.

The rain eased just as he drained the last of his Starbucks from the bottom of the cup, he popped open his door, and stepped out into the light drizzle. He grabbed his black leather BOSS bag from the back seat, stepped over the small pothole by the rear tyre and headed towards the entrance. The 1980s theme continued with the intercom, memories of doctors visits as a child came flooding back as he pressed the faded yellow button marked reception. The crackled voice greeted him, and buzzed him through.

They clearly hadn't wanted to deviate from the theme inside. Mottled grey carpet tiles corner to corner, finished with scuffed black rubber edging that had seen better days. Some kind soul had decided to layer up a few more carpet tiles to act as a doormat for days such as this. The entranceway furniture appeared to be standard order oak laminate, straight out of an office catalogue. Reception desk, tables, chairs, each with it's own unique chip and scuff. Yellowing paint adorned the peeling wallpaper, a poor attempt at a low cost spruce up many year ago.

"Mornin' pal!" came the jovial greeting.

A scruffy haired, spindly man leaning over the reception desk, clearly in heavy conversation with the young receptionist. The man was likely in his early 40s, but his unkempt appearance, greying sideburns, and creased corporate polo shirt pegged him nearer 50. The receptionist, however, a curvy 20-something brunette, did not seem as interested in the conversation as he was.

A few cordial greetings later established the pair as Steph who duly logged him in the visitors book, whilst handing him a lanyard to wear around the building.

She then set about calling Steve's first meeting of the day. Visibly grateful to be relieved of her conversation with the man who now introduced himself as Colin.

"Part of the facilities team, well I say team, just me and Baz on a Thursday and Friday!" he chuckled.

Steve knew to keep these guys sweet, the engine of any office environment, he was going to need a few things doing, and these guys would be doing lots of the heavy lifting. He turned on the charm, and made sure that in this instance, the first impression was a good one. Keeping the conversation flowing, and feigning interest in air conditioning developments for the building, until his contact arrived.

The following couple of hours were spent with the cheerful Maggie from HR. A company lifer, with over 34 years service. Her husband worked upstairs in logistics. They had met here 30 years ago, and married the same year. More small talk flowed as they ran through the standard protocols of the company, signing document after document. Most people would find this tiring and meaningless, however, for someone as insightful as Steve, it gave him sight of the political playbook. A clear picture of where the power and influence resided. Disproportionate quantities of procedures and policies for departments such as IT, meant that their Director, Phil Bolton, a 52-year old Scot, was moved up a few pegs on the charm list. He wasn't heir to the throne, nor kingmaker, nor strategic wizard, that was not where his value lay. However, what was clear from the first couple of hours spent autographing like Beckham in a book store, was that he had the place tied up in bureaucracy and administrative authority. Failing to acknowledge this, and court the Glaswegian, could play out as a difficulty in obtaining equipment, access to systems, and ending up at the back of any job sheet workflows. All of which would hamper Steve's ability to be first.

The term 'office' was used very loosely for Maggie's converted stationary cupboard. The poor cat would have suffered severe head trauma had it dare be swung in the space. So lunchtime was welcome respite, as the temperature and humidity in the room were becoming untenable. A short, tour-guided, stroll to the office canteen led him past the facilities office, where Colin was tapping single fingered on his keyboard. Maggie served to introduce him for the second time, as well as Rebecca from HR who was patiently waiting for him to arrange some postage.

"Nice guy that! Nice guy!" Steve overheard as the tour left its stop, and moved onwards. He smiled to himself.

Finally, they reached the canteen, at the end of a long winding corridor. Maggie waved to her husband, and headed over to introduce Steve. As they walked, Steve felt a hand on his shoulder, and turned to see John Russell. His big powerful hand outstretched, with another one in waiting to slap onto Steve's forearm. The power shake that many in the industry knew so well. Matched with the piercing blue eyed stare, you could easily see why this man had struck many a good trade deal in the last few decades. The interaction took Maggie somewhat by surprise, clearly intimidated by the power that Russell wielded around the building, she struggled to comprehend the visibly warm relationship between Steve and the company founder.

The trio parted, as Russell excused himself to meet with new investors. Something Steve remembered to this day, the look in Russell's eyes, a painful resignation even then, that his business, his creation, was being edged away from him. A moment lost on those around them, but something he knew to log in the recesses of his memory. Something he hoped wouldn't remain in his memory, however, was the taste of the so called Premium Fish and Chips from the lunch menu. Clearing up, he gave a courteous nod and smile to the cashier when asked how it was. This was one relationship he wouldn't be working the charm for, and resolved there and then to get lunch from the Shell station on the drive in.

Maggie was keen to continue her guided tour of the premises. Reenergised by the impression that the tall, stocky gentleman she was introducing to everyone, was clearly so close to the higher authorities. With over 200 people employed in the building, Steve wasn't sure how he was expected to remember every name, let alone the various personal fact files that Maggie reeled off. Nevertheless, he played his role perfectly, never deviating from his well rehearsed routines. Humble, kind, and warm were certainly not words from his resume or references, however he had been comfortable in their skin over the next few hours of that first day.

The knock at the door bought him back from his reminiscing, almost exactly coinciding with the tuneful ding of his iPad. Both of which notifying that his 9.30 meeting was due to begin.

"Yep!" he beckoned.

A timid Ian Andrews entered the room. Steve remained behind the large walnut desk, rolling slightly back on his large leather chair. Chest puffed out, and arms folded, it didn't take a body language guru to see that this wasn't going to be pleasant for Andrews. He had never liked the man who had been quite a vocal dissenter of Steve's most recent promotion only weeks ago.

"Morning Steve, good evening?" Blurted the nervous Regional Manager.

"Had better." came the dismissive retort, twinned with Steve outstretching his arm to place the printed out email just short of Andrews' view.

"Is that the Doncaster issue? I've spoken to…" the pace and blurting running into the impending cut off.

"I don't really give a shit about who you've spoken to Ian. The customer broke her fucking leg." The expletives delivered relatively low level. Allowing his body language, and the facts to resonate.

The man standing in front of him was already intimidated. Being asked, just the day before, to drive 150 miles for a 30 minute meeting with Steve Bellingham was enough. The long drive down, packed with self-talk, and practice speeches to try and placate the COO.

"Yeah, it's awful, we've spoken to her family, and they aren't pressing charges." delivered with contrived confidence.

"And you believe that? You think that makes it all OK? She broke her fucking leg Ian," He paused for effect. "and it's your team's fault."

"Yes, I know, I didn't want to, I mean, I wanted to try and not worry you." stumbling himself into knots.

Steve took a long, deep, intake of breath. He would have gone to the coffee to prolong his pain, but it was definitely cold by now.

"I'm dealing with the Manager, and the Area Manager, she's on holiday, but as soon as she's back I'll sort it Steve." He stuttered, desperate for the silence to end.

"You were there the day before and you didn't notice anything wrong?"

Andrews shuffled uncomfortably on his feet, glancing longingly at the chairs around the large meeting table in the room. Desperate to sit and hide the shakes in 2 of his limbs.

"I'm sorry Steve, I'll sort it."

"You've said that Ian. Come on, you've been doing this long enough." He was right, Ian Andrews was one of the longest serving people at the company, nearly 45 years. The reference was not placed for respect of his service however.

"Yep, you're right." He sighed in heavy acknowledgment. Any residual confidence in the older man was draining out of him. His head dropped momentarily to look at the carpet like a scolded schoolboy.

"I want the Manager, and A.M. dealt with immediately." He glanced out of the window to the sun filled gardens below "What would you do if you were in my shoes?"

"No different, Steve. I should have done something about it." referring to the loose paving stone that caused the customer to fall out of the shop entrance.

"Ian, man the fuck up and think about your place in this. Neglect. Failure to keep customers safe. Not a good way to end a career."

Resignation visibly swept through Andrews body. Noticeable also was a mild relief. The uncomfortableness had subsided, the nervous movements stopped. More confident in his skin and what was approaching next.

"It's over isn't it?"

"If you think so Ian." This was almost too easy.

"How can I retire? I mean I've still got my house, and my wife will..." The floodgates of consciousness opened.

"It's ultimately your decision Ian, but I need to know now, otherwise I'll be working up the disciplinary paperwork with Martin."

Andrews eye roll at the mention of Martin Armstrong was masked by a close of his eyes and deep breath.

"OK, give me a few days and I'll sort, I mean I'll let you know. I need to talk to my other half."

Steve had no intention of working up this paperwork, knowing that Andrews' relationship with the Retail Director Armstrong was poor. Especially following his vocal dissent previously. Armstrong was Steve's man, and this had marked Andrews' card months ago. So much so, that the retirement notification was the only paperwork being worked up.

"I understand. Let Martin know. I want the other dealt with, or I will be forced to take this further."

"It'll be done by weekend Steve, you have my word."

"I want to know the outcomes immediately after. Look, there's nothing else. I need to talk to Martin." dismissed the COO.

"Right, OK, I'll head back up north. Thanks Steve, I'll ring you end of the week with an update."

"Cheers Ian, close the door on the way out." and with that, done. Ending a nigh on 45 year career of a man 20 years his senior. It had taken a while to find the catalyst, until it practically fell into his lap.

However, the lack of challenge and chance to stretch his cognitive functions left him a little underwhelmed. Wondering if this was getting a bit easy. Only minor tidying up would be needed. Andrews had been close to John Russell given his length of time in the company, so this would need to be managed, in no more than a phone call. The rest would flow.

As the door shut, Steve took a minute, before picking up his phone. First, a quick text to his PA asking for a fresh coffee. The next, punching in the Retail Director's name, and pressing call.

"Martin, it's Steve. He's taking retirement. No real issue" short, and to the point.

"Cheers boss, he's ringing me now." he chuckled. The plan moving at greater pace than expected.

"K, chat later." signing off barely seconds into the call.

He knew he needed to give it a while for this to work through the system before calling Russell. With the half hour meeting complete in just over half that time, he took the opportunity to check his emails once more. His requested meeting had been booked in, and there was relatively little of note in the inbox, with the exception of one.

Security and GDPR Breaches.

This is a reminder to all colleagues, that company emails are not to be moved to private servers or forwarded to private email addresses. This risks a considerable and serious risk to the security of the company, as well as a potential breach of GDPR policy.

With this in mind, the IT team have updated both policies, and attached them below. Please ensure you have read, signed and returned these to your Line Manager by close of play Wednesday.

Thank you,

Phil

Phil Bolton

IT Director

Russell's Retail

Phil did love a policy to sign. Steve mused. The IT Director had been a long term ally, a carefully constructed, and controlled ally at that. They had met at the end of Steve's first day. The IT department had been last on the list for Maggie's tour. Primarily, given its location in one of the office outbuildings. Maggie had explained that they had moved out there a few months after Bolton had joined. It hadn't taken much to establish this key part of his psychology. Therefore, it was no surprise that opening the door revealed a far more modern interior than that of the main building. Brand new air conditioning units humming happily on the wall, no chipped laminate wood effect desks in sight, wall to wall were banks of clean and white with modern screens, Steve even noticed a couple of part bitten apples shining against the grey metal on the corner desks.

Bolton had come out of his large glass walled office to greet them. His Glaswegian accent had softened in the years south of the border, but there were still threads of it. Enough for Steve to pull for reaction, allowing them to spend time discussing some of the bars around Ingram Street, the recent footballing upturn of the blue side of the city, as well as a shared pain of the local airport. The Director had taken up the tour from this point, playing clearly into Steve's hands. He was Laird of this land, and spoke with fiery passion about how this converted cow shed was now one of the finest retail IT departments in the UK. This may have been some stretch of the imagination, but Steve was certainly not going to dissuade, far from it, he even fanned those flames a little stronger for effect.

The relationship had continued to build through the last couple of years. Bolton a strong supporter of Steve in board meetings. He was also the first person to call and congratulate both his promotion to Retail Director, and recent one to Chief Operating Officer. Steve had played his part here too. Regularly ensuring that all IT obligations were fulfilled from his team, and always being a front line advocate of the way things were conducted technically and digitally.

Steve fired back a short response to his colleague.

"Consider mine done by Friday." and by copying in those directly in his teams, the bar had been set.

Fresh cup of coffee in hand, he commenced his daily walk through the building. Something he had always done since only his second day. Preferring that those around the company saw him. The lower level staff liked this, and felt like he was approachable and engaging. Dispelling some myth about him not liking small talk. Management teams however, felt on edge, skin prickled by the sight of him entering their department, backs straightened if he made eye contact. A perfect balance, when struck right.

One of his key domains, and final stop on the tour, was the trading department. A team of over 50 product buyers ensuring the fundamentals of a retail business were delivered. Buy a product from a supplier and sell it for more. Years ago, you would never believe the amount of people that were now sat in this part of the building. As he walked past the first bank of desks, he could hear negotiations with suppliers, one in particular, getting quite heated about the cost price of mayonnaise.

The department was led by Mark Jeffries, another company lifer. Another of the old school. After, just over 30 years service, he expected to be first in line for the COO role. He now needed to remain content with his Trading Director title, and reporting into the man who had bested him. Jeffries was capable, sure, but his inability to play the political game was his downfall. However, Russell was very protective of the ex-soldier, especially following his issues with alcohol just before Steve joined. He had fallen off the wagon at a company conference, slurring his words and stumbling on stage in the middle of the afternoon, and had to be supported back to his hotel by the company founder and the previous COO. With the right help, he had overcome his demons.

Sadly, he had then came across as resentful and bitter when realising Steve was up against him for the job. Rumour had it, he had stormed into John Russell's office to have it out with him. Something Steve never witnessed, but had no reason to refute. This had stirred rumours of his previous issues with the bottle, and Russell simply could not appoint him in that spotlight.

"Mark. Morning. All OK for tomorrow?"

No real need to firm up the timings, but he knew it wound Jeffries up being summoned to meetings in such a way.

"Uh huh." Jeffries barely lifted his head from over the shoulder of one of the buyers. "Q3 projections yeah?"

"Please. I'm not happy with the first draft the boys showed me earlier." referring to the duo from finance who were tasked with putting the year's sales budget together.

"Right. OK." resigned Mark. Knowing any discourse at this stage would be pointless. Steve would show him up in front of his relatively loyal team, he preferred to bite his tongue until later.

"Cheers." Steve read him like a book, and now had him riled up for the rest of the day. Meaning he would be driven by emotion in their later meeting, rather than calm, controlled, logic like the man now walking away.

To the uninformed observer, their relationship would have appeared functional at best, maybe a little frosty. However, behind scenes, the frost certainly melted. Many a fiery meeting had been held in both their offices in the few weeks since the change in leadership. Things were still very raw.

"Excuse me, Steve?" came a confident voice from the desk to his right. "can I just check something with you?"

The rare request startled him slightly, and he turned to see the relatively new face of Lucy the buyer for crisps. An attractive brunette in her late 20s, recently engaged, if Steve remember correctly.

"Of course, what's up?" regaining his composure. Out of the corner of his eye, he could see Mark's attention was piqued.

"Finance have just sent these back for review, asking for increases." she pointed at the recently received email open on her screen. Leaning in, he noted the tone in which it had been sent. This would be dealt with later.

"I'm already over what I think I can get." she exclaimed boldly.

"One to pick up with Mark." Steve deflected. He should be picking up this mess with his team. Standing to leave her desk.

"But it says you are asking for more." Boldness, turning brash. Eyes raised above the other monitors on the desks surrounding them. "I know others will feel the same."

"Lucy, is it?" Condescension was necessary, Steve deemed. To put this little upstart in her place if nothing else. "as a public company, we have expectations. Shareholder expectations. We cannot. Absolutely cannot report low numbers this year."

"And if we don't hit them? Then what?" She continued. Mark Jeffries slowly approached closer.

"Pick it up with Mark." His chest tightened in frustration, teeth gritted "Run through it with him. Talk to your suppliers. We need more. End of."

He moved to leave, casting a strong, firm eye at Mark Jeffries who was now at the scene in heavy discussion with the member of his team. This would be raised tomorrow. No doubt.

2

....

"Morning boss! Congratulations on the promotion!" instantly recognisable cheer from Colin the facilities man. Tanned, but with white flaking skin, belying a peeling red nose. Clearly from his recent holiday. "Well deserved I say! Very well deserved!"

"Morning Colin, thanks pal! Been a few weeks now! Cheers for sorting my air con by the way." reciprocated Steve.

"No worries at all boss, anything for you!" As he went on his merry way, screwdriver in hand. Eyes led by the young, female financier climbing the stairs ahead of him.

The promotion to COO had been no surprise to anyone in the building. There was really no serious choice as far as everyone could see, bar a couple of the old timers. By this point, he was the heartbeat of the company, pulling the strings, and injecting much needed adrenaline wherever he went. He had dealt with many of his detractors, and roadblocks along the way. There was still more to do here if he was to fully realise his ambitions, but for now, things were going to plan.

His equity rose as they took the company to floatation. Driving the performance of many areas to new levels, working day and night to do so. Financially, the initial investors, and those around the company, benefitted from the early climbs in the price of stock. All of which placed the credit firmly at his office door. This had earned him the right to be front runner for the job when it was announced Tom O'Donnell, his predecessor, was retiring. Calls from editors and journos, were coming in days before it was officially announced to the city. All looking for a scoop. His carefully worded retorts to the right outlets had given them plenty to work with, and duly the message was a positive one, even if it needed a little massaging along the way.

Another small bump in value gave everyone around the company the confidence that this was the right appointment. Especially those with larger stakes than others. John Russell in particular, had been only too glad to see the back of his friend, and previous COO, if this was the small windfall he was going to get with Steve at the helm of the day to day business.

On this bright sunny morning, just like any other, Steve arrived early. Preferring to be one of the first in, most didn't arrive until at least 8am. It was only really Colin, now back from holiday, busy making his rounds, delivering the post to various offices, and whistling a nondescript tune whilst checking on the ageing building infrastructure. One of the few people in this office that Steve genuinely liked, he did his job without fuss. Never complaining about the lack of resources or things asked of him. Some people are just naturally happy with their lot, never striving for more. From what Steve knew about him, he was a single man, divorced, living in a flat in the centre of town. How life was different for the two men, not so dissimilar in age.

Steve on the other hand was a man of possessions and achievement. Belief that success was judged in the eye of the beholder, drove him to buy more, and buy bigger. Pushing him to work harder, and smarter. He was a corporate capitalism golden boy if ever there was one. The Starbucks cup, the leather bag, the gleaming black Jaguar. On his right wrist, his stunning new Rolex Submariner continued the look. A wonderful wedding anniversary present. Sadly, from his own bank account. Glancing proudly at it, he realised he was a little early this morning, even by his own standards. Only just after 7am.

He was very surprised, therefore, to see the rear view of Mark Jeffries waiting outside his office at such an hour.

"We need to talk." he demanded. Barely waiting for the office door to be unlocked.

"Morning to you too!" unlocking the old oak door awkwardly. Opening up to the large corner office that came with the new title.

The room was relatively bare for his liking. With only weeks in the position, he hadn't got his stamp on it. Eventually, the room would be painted, his bookcase relocated, along with his favourite selection of display-only business books. Positioned carefully alongside his small selection of awards. Much work to do, but still imposed a sense of hierarchical superiority in its fabric alone. How Mark Jeffries longed for the roles to be reversed at this point.

"Grab a seat." Steve signalled to one of the simple chairs around his large oval meeting table. He opted for perching on the corner of his desk.

"These numbers are impossible Steve, the guys just can't get another three percent out." emotion and frustration leading his words. Jealousy clearly in his eyes, looking up towards Steve a few feet away.

"Do you want to go tell John that? Or shall I?" the gauntlet thrown at his opponent.

"Fuck's sake Steve. You've got the job already. Q1 was shit. We are miles off Q2 now, on your advice I'll add. Now you're telling me to raise again for Q3. I'll get my bollocks handed to me!"

"It's not my fault you're missing the Q2 numbers." Steve opted to dodge the early taunt to engage.

"You can sit there all you like and throw it around, but you pushed that plan through, and now you're doing it again. I don't know what your game is, but I'm not playing it!" gesticulating like a temper stricken child.

"Mark, calm down. You know how this works. Q2 will come up short. Now that's your team's failing. Nobody else. Everyone expects, and needs, us to make that back in three." The physical and psychological higher ground was certainly Steve's preferred positioning.

"Put in what you fucking like, the team are not happy, and know they can't do it!" Mark shifted, uncomfortable in his seat. as red mist descended around him.

"Throwing them under the bus now? Anything to save your arse in front of John? Get a grip Mark." Steve couldn't resist. "It's your plan, but I'm being really clear on my expectations here and now. Deliver the number I'm asking you to."

"I knew it wouldn't take long." exasperated Mark, throwing himself back in his chair before standing, and pointing at Steve

"Didn't take much for you to start throwing your weight around. You've been here 5 minutes and you think you know how it all works. Got all the answers.

Well I don't know who's dick you sucked to get this." further gesticulation around the room.

"Mark. Stop. I suggest you watch your words right now. Or this will be a different conversation." now he was firmly under Jeffries' skin.

"Fuck you Steve, you'll get your fucking budget!" and with that he stormed to the door and with a bluster of heavy huffs, slammed it behind him. Shaking dust from the loose light fitting above the table.

It took every ounce of self restraint from Steve to not chase him down the long corridor. In his younger, more tempestuous days, he would have had the grey-haired man up by his throat, resolving things in the extremely short term. However, now he knew this only worsened things in the medium and long term, and took it out on his desk instead. Expletives filling the air.

He rose to the window, taking a long deep breath. Not the start to the day he had envisaged. He hadn't even had the chance to rebuke him over the outspoken upstart in his department.

Looking down the lane to the horizon, he knew there was truth in Mark's venom. The Q2 targets had been pushed up, his previously agreeable relationship with Mark had guided him to such. Whilst it wasn't directly on Steve's head, he was certainly more culpable than the man now bashing through swing doors at a rate of knots. It was Steve who had convinced his predecessor to put the pressure on for the bigger number when the profit targets were first being set over 6 months ago.

As planned, these projections had been well received by the city. Perfectly positioned ready for O'Donnell to exit and Steve to step in, both benefitting financially in the process.

A familiar rat-a-tat at the door meant that Charlotte had arrived, letting herself in, hot coffee in hand.

"Morning boss." she greeted tentatively, clearly not used to seeing him stood staring out of a window. "everything alright?"

"Thanks love, yeah. Yeah, all good." drifting back to the moment.

"Mark's booked in for 8. Do you…"

"Already been in." Steve interrupted.

"Oh OK." clearly caught off guard, but quickly realising this was likely the reason for his distant manner "I need to talk to you about something."

Oh great. Steve mused. A morning of people needing to talk to me in this way can never be positive.

"I'm leaving." like ripping off a plaster, she felt instant relief.

"Oh wow, OK." slight more of a reaction than Steve expected to give away "That's a shame"

"Thanks, yeah I got something better in town. Er, I mean different." she stumbled.

"It's fine. I understand." he chuckled, some light relief to the morning "So what is it, a week's notice now?"

"Please if that's OK, gives me a few days before starting in the new place, nearer home n'all." she continued

"They already got a new girl lined up for ya." now the shackles of a formal working relationship were off, her more natural patter was seeping through.

"Fair enough, I'll call the agency later to firm it up then. Thanks for telling me, it's been a decent few months. Not sure the new girl's coffee will be as good as yours!" He lied. The stuff she made tasted like ground horse shit, but no point knocking the poor girl off her stride. He had bigger battles.

"Aww thanks." a slight rosy blush came over her fair skin "I'll send her some instructions or summit!"

"Good plan. Thanks." Steve tried to pull the conversation to a halt, ending any eye contact by glancing at his watch, then less subtly grabbling his bag from the floor and unzipping it. Charlotte wasn't the brightest, but clearly got the hint.

"Er, yeah so if you need anything I'll be next door. Thanks for understanding though. It's been alright really." she smiled, correcting her top before turning to leave.

"Thanks Charlotte, pop the door will you." Steve instructed, barely lifting his eyes from unpacking.

He sat. Sipped the lukewarm brown liquid in his favoured mug. She had done alright in the time she was here. Not cocked too much up, he thought. The morning had taken a mildly unexpected turn, but a very minor detour would not hamper his progress. There was no point fighting to keep his PA, just because she hadn't caused him many issues. She was young, and needed to find her way. Another one would be off the line any time soon. A few weeks of making sure she doesn't destroy stuff, and it'll be like things never changed.

He popped open his iPad, clumsily folding the stand underneath at the third attempt. Tapped in his passcode and headed straight to the daily sales details. Nothing spectacular, just steadily average, however, as the earlier encounter had put it so eloquently, they were miles off target for this quarter.

No reaction passed his face. He moved to check the share price, which raised a slight eyebrow. The mild decline of the recent ten or so days was continuing, and like the brow of the hills in the distance, it was beginning to steepen. Not something it had seen since the floatation, but was to be expected, he reflected.

The next hour was filled with benign administrative tasks. This banausic side of the job was sadly necessary. Authorising his team's expenses, filing his own, and keeping tabs on some of their reporting. All part of oiling the machine. Stuff that couldn't be delegated, even to a strong PA.

However, the morning improved for him somewhat, seeing that almost all his team had signed their IT documents and returned them. Including Mark Jeffries in the last few moments. He had expected him to spoil his ballot, but maybe he was wrong about the man.

"Morning Steve," the door opened "all alright?"

Jane Thorne was never one to knock. JT, as she was more commonly known around here, was the effervescent HR Director, although she preferred the title Director of Colleague Wellness. Even the thought of it turned Steve's stomach, as much as her permanent smile, and sickly sweet persona did the same. She would almost skip around the office at any given opportunity. Gladly spending inordinate amounts of time chatting, just to make sure everyone was "all alright".

To her credit, she commanded any room she entered, a shade over five foot eight in heels, always dressed in immaculate, tailored suiting. Steve admired this about her, a rare concession, bordering on respect. Even if she did stand out like a Prada store on a Hull council estate.

"JT, my lovely, how are you this morning?" Leaning in, fully expecting the double cheek kiss, and getting a strong intake of her expensive perfume.

"Wonderful my darling. The sun is shining." you could almost taste the rainbow "Although MJ wasn't a happy camper just now."

Her fondness of acronymic names, was ironic, given that she had dropped her own occupationally titled one, and at times, made it feel more like a venereal disease centre than a retail business.

She had clearly bumped into a firecracker Mark Jeffries on her way to her weekly, regular, one to one with the COO.

"Struggling with the new regime I would say. It's tough for him." Steve tried to play him into the resentful, but troubled, teenager box.

"Although, you know, I am quite concerned about him recently."

She pulled a chair from around the table to be sat at the side of Steve's corner desk. Stretching out her long pale legs, tipped with bright red, patent, Louboutins. Only slightly redder than her curled locks, that she was now elaborately flinging back, eyes to the ceiling in dramatic thought.

"I shared this worry with John." Russell was the only person obviated from an acronym

"Appointing you was the right move, but clearly was going to upset MJ."

"Very grateful for the support." allowing himself a grin "I'll sit him down later for a chat, clear the air and all."

The two went on to discuss various low level people issues within Steve's new jurisdictions. Potential superstar performers and those who needed that little bit extra rocket up their backsides.

"Sadly, I think Ian Andrews is going to retire, he rang Martin yesterday. Says the travelling is just getting too much, and given what happened last week." Nonchalantly skipping any detail of yesterdays meeting "I think we should do something for him."

"Wonderful idea, I'll get Mags on the case." She paused, checking her phone briefly before standing, and dusting off her navy two piece "Well, if there's nothing else my love, I must be getting on!"

"Pleasure as always." Steve stood, knowing the old fashioned manners still held favour with his well to do colleague. This relationship had served him well over the years, and would be needed, more than ever, going forward.

As she was leaving, Steve's phone buzzed in his pocket. He pulled it out to see the caller ID. He declined the call, and flicked through to the messages function.

Can't talk right now

He dialled the number he had saved for Office Diamonds local rep. Luckily Charlotte had done her bit, and informed them of her intentions the previous day, and as promised, they already had a replacement lined up. Timing had worked in his favour clearly. Whilst he did not want to lose Charlotte deep down, especially after only a couple of months, and her having been there through his promotion, the opportunity to bring someone in, learning the new role from scratch had its appeal. Especially given the quality of the CV that had just arrived in his email inbox.

Handover plans were roughly outlined, leaving the finer detail for Charlotte and the rep, the key thing for

Steve was getting good cross over of the two individuals. Easily agreed given the extortionate annual fees for such service. It was agreed that the new PA would be able to meet up for an introduction in the coming days.

Charlotte had never reached the inner circle of Steve's trust. Very few ever did, let alone those on the payroll here. In fact, only two people at Russell's were considered worthy. One of which, was Martin Armstrong, now Retail Director following Steve's promotion. A loyal and willing number two, he had been bought in during Steve's time in the same role. Armstrong was barely 32 when he was introduced into the company, the young firebrand ruffled many feathers on his first few months. Mainly at the behest of his mentor and line manager. This in truth, was his best talent. As whilst he was savvy on a spreadsheet, a gifted orator, and a keen social strategist, above all he was Steve's allegiant attack-dog. Following him around his last two companies, there was no surprise when he was fished over to join Russell's. His unwavering loyalty manifested almost instantaneously upon their first meeting. Armstrong knew which side his bread was buttered, and where the ham, and then the cheese was going to come from, and so duly delivered.

The trend continued to this day. Generally, Steve making the flashed decision, and Armstrong executing with ruthless effect.

All complete.

Read the email, above an attachment entitled 'I.Andrews - Leaver Form - Retirement'. Steve opened it, and as expected, he noted the only reasons for leaving as 'length of travel'. A few more trips from Doncaster to Stevenage for a disciplinary would have confirmed that to him.

This movement of personnel also now allowed another of Steve's pack to be leashed up. Martin was already a step ahead of him as always, as he signed the email off to confirm he was working on replacing him. More weight on his side of the scales, he smiled.

The journey to tipping the scales once and for all in his favour was, rightly, long and arduous. Picking off the dissenters and misfits too quick would be conspicuous. Too slow and he himself would be left behind. The correct pace to removing the rot was vital. One of the largest remaining cankers had spread deeper in this morning. This needed resolving. He had promised the Princess of People he would put his arm around his disgruntled Director, he just hadn't confirmed where, or how tight.

The vision of this was in his head as he approached Jeffries office. A long, thin slither carved out of the trading department floor. Like a leech on the side of the office, draining the only natural light feeding into this part of the building. Stuffed with a continuation of the company's cheap laminate furniture catalogue. The perceivable temporary nature, of a room made in such a way, was lost on its inhabitant. Steve's desire now, was that his reputation, and career, was as easy to deconstruct.

He looked through the one glass panel of the office wall, to see Jeffries, feet crossed up on the desk, staring out of his long open window. His phone glued to his right ear, left arm waving around as if conducting a Rachmaninov piano concerto. Vigorous, mumbled, conversation could barely be made out despite the thin partition walls. Steve stood, and watched, until eventually, he was noticed. A flicker of a raised eyebrow meant he knew he'd been caught, and a microcosm of emotions clearly ripped through him in milliseconds. His prostrate positioning so out of character, he wondered if it was as obvious that his phone call was also. Momentarily wondering if he should contract back, or not.

Two fingers were raised. Palm forward. Clearly not denoting the peace sign, but signalling he required a further two minutes. Before turning back to the window. There were not many reactions Jeffries could have pulled in that moment that would have placated Steve. This one, a sign of nonchalant defiance, though, was highly reactive. He let himself into the office, closing the door behind him, which caused an almost comical retrench of position from the Trading Director, and a hurried close to his phone call, promising to call its recipient later.

Steve moved to sit on the corner of the rectangular meeting table. He attempted to hide a flinch, as the unstable leg creaked and veered slightly to his right.

"Guess it's urgent?" defiantly defending his position "That was Saj from Sixtrees"

"Mark, we need to chat." ignoring the barefaced lie, for now.

"Do we? I think I was pretty clear this morning. You'll get your numbers." His normally composed pale complexion, was now a pinkish blotchy flush.

"Let's be really honest for a moment, I'd get them if you're in that chair or not." Calm and controlled, so not to be deemed as a threat, he continued "You have control of this team, you are their leader. They are a loyal bunch."

"No doubt there." Jeffries interjected, looking out the window to his hardworking troupe.

"They respect you." that word meant so much to the man. So much, his face began to return to pale instantaneously "So you storming around this place like a child erodes that."

There was silence. Almost as if all work outside had ceased.

"A child? Christ Steve, I'm old enough to…"

"Be my father, yes, we've been here before Mark. But it needs to calm down. If we can't work together, then I will find someone else. Right now, I need you." Steve hid his gritted teeth through the last statement.

The small white lie had the desired effect on Jeffries, still staring through the window.

"I need you Mark. I'm new to this, and need you, and your team on my side. It's not going to be easy, I get that. But you know this place better than anyone." Steve continued, suppressing his need to be completely honest.

Clearly lost for words, Jeffries could barely look him in the eye. His gaze moved slowly across the room, until it was wistfully fixed on the singular cedar tree scraping the window pane on the other side. He felt he had won.

"I'm not apologising," he returned "but I get it. I'll get back in my box."

"Mark, I appreciate it, you're a good man." Steve needed to leave before his coffee made a return back where it came from.

The two shook hands. Jeffries right hand was cold but clammy. A combination of the cheap plastic handset, and anger induced fist clenching. Steve exited, and closed the door behind. The group of buyers nearest the office door scurried their eyes back to their screens, like mice who had seen the house cat return.

As he left the office, Steve fired off a quick text, and made his way through the rest of the department. He smiled at Lucy, who had triggered much of this yesterday, but he was comfortable in the way the last few minutes had gone. He wanted, no, needed, Mark Jeffries out the way, but bludgeoning a fellow board member out the way was not the approach. This needed finesse and craft. His phone pinged.

From: Saj - Sixtrees.

No boss, not heard from him in weeks

He clicked his phone shut, placed it back in his pocket and gathered pace back to his office.

3

Steve was not a big fan of weekends. The hustle, bustle and constant tussle of the working week was what gave him life, but also strangely, relaxed him. Maybe it was the pace he worked at, or the synaptic demands he put upon his mind, but the abrupt two day slowdown seemed to agitate him. God help his wife, Sarah, on a Bank Holiday weekend. His failure to want to switch off causing mutual frustration. They were not big socialisers, adventurers, or proud home makers. So weekends lacked a focus, and shared sense of enjoyment.

They had been together 15 years, next year, married just over 11. A richly burning initial romance, had dwindled to a light flicker over the decade of wedlock. Occasionally erupting into a full blown furnace, but these moments were getting fewer and farther between. It was the arguments that burnt them both more now.

There was no classic fairytale as to how they had met. Convergent groups of friends on a night out led them to slurred conversation over the emphatic sound system. A strong physical attraction, and good conversation was the foundation of their marriage a few years later. The modern day conveyor belt relationship. Her inability to have children caused them only minor upset in earlier years. For differing reasons, both were content in their forced decision on the subject.

As Steve progressed in his career, Sarah saw less and less need to work. A lifestyle they both found comfort in. He got to come home to relative order and peace, at many times of the evening. She got a deep pool of a bank account in which to take a daily swim. Much was not shared between them, other than a regular transfer of funds into the credit card.

The decision to relocate from Royal Leamington Spa to Northampton had been Steve's, and his alone. Sarah knew she would not have much case to fight to stay. Besides, she would be able to make more friends, and the shops were a bit better in that area anyway. The large 5 bedroom place they now owned there, had been surprisingly in their budget. Steve had insisted so. Financially, Sarah rarely asked questions, preferring to enjoy its presence, than ask where it came from, despite the fact there appeared to be more around than she expected.

Most weekends went by just as this one had, late starts, coffee out and about, and returning with bags of shopping. Occasionally seeing some of Sarah's friends in the evening, avoided where possible by Steve. These tended to be very one sided affairs. Numbing conversation with a bunch of filled shirts with elevated egos, interspersed by the checking of emails and taking occasional non-urgent calls.

Therefore, it was a welcome return for Steve this Monday morning, as he pulled into the car park. Passing the spot he used on his very first day, now pulling around the front to his designated spot. To save money, Colin had sprayed a couple of lines to section off the three spaces. Each marked with the three letter acronyms for those who were permitted to park here. CEO, COO and CFO. Steve's 3 week old, specced out Jaguar XJ was more suited to this location, nestled in nicely behind the Land Rover Defender.

The registration plate JR 123 was as iconic as the man's razor short ginger hair, or powerful handshake. The handshake that was now reaching out to greet Steve on this breezy morning.

"Morning Steven, good weekend I trust?" the deep Yorkshire baritone echoed off the concrete clad walls, as he stepped down from his vehicle. "Lovely motor, that new?"

"Thanks John, benefit of not having kids." he called, grabbing his bag from the rear seat

"You're a lucky man, mine bleed me for every penny." he chortled "Shame about Andrews, fine man, but I guess it's the right time eh?"

By now, Steve knew the reality behind the jaunty, carefree conversational tone of the rotund man, almost six inches shorter, now walking alongside him. Never missing a trick, and always having a knack of delving into information. A technique that had got him to his elevated position today. Revered, feared, but ultimately respected. He had a style that no management book, or thousand pound leadership course could impart, and he was damn effective with it.

"Very, he was just getting a step off the pace. Mags is throwing a proper do for him." No point engaging around the issues Andrews was causing in meetings with his loose opinions and even looser jaw.

"Ah top stuff, good, good. All set for this morning?" he deflected as they entered the building side by side.

"Always, and I'll be good this week." referring to his vocal disagreement of the changing of lead food wholesaler last week. "Catch you at ten."

"Thank you, Steven." Russell climbed the stairs towards his top floor office, leaving Steve behind. He could see the old man's knowing, almost cheeky, grin as he disappeared.

The standard weekly board meeting to which he had referred was the highlight of the Monday calendar for most. Steve enjoyed the arid, lifeless nature of it. Making him appear even more capable and exciting.

Steve considered the nine other Directors sat around the large boardroom. Only a couple were real business minds, nobody sharp enough to outwit, or outsmart him. Generally nose deep in the presentation paraphernalia trying to make sense of whatever was being asked of them.

It was good to have Martin Armstrong sat across from him now, another strong and fearless support in the room, working as a pincer movement across the large expanse of mahogany. JT did her part on the whole, rarely disagreeing with Steve unless it stepped into her domain, in which he rarely ventured. Russell was no real challenge in this environment either, as disconnected to the day to day running as a 62-year old founder should be. He would be swayed by the room, although generally carrying more weight in his longer term compatriots view. Very occasionally vehemently agreeing or disagreeing with a proposal.

This meeting was as uneventful as most, although a glance at the agenda suggested the controversial subject of wholesale contract was listed just after their break for lunch. Martin nodded at him across the table in acknowledgment of this. This was strange, as it had been quashed at the last meeting as far as Steve was concerned.

"Supply back on the table then boss?" Martin hushed in his ear as they selected their chosen triangle sandwiches from the supermarket bought platter selection in front of them.

"Never understand why we can't make our own sandwiches." he responded, with a flick of the head to suggest they take their conversation to the corner of the room.

"Sorry boss." Martin hurriedly excused himself.

"It's fine, I can't understand why it's back either. John was funny about it this morning. Let me see what I can work out." aware that Mark Jeffries was attempting a casual looking snoop in their direction.

As Trading Director, this was Jeffries' remit. Everything to do with suppliers went through him and his team. Whilst Steve was staunchly against a switch, for reasons he kept completely to himself, he had allowed Jeffries to get this on the agenda previously. A move that he hoped was appreciated, an attempt to keep him sweet in his new role. The conversation needed to be had, certain non-executives and investors had been pushing the point for a while. So as far as Steve was concerned, this could be two dead birds, with one tiny pebble. However, somehow, it was back on the agenda. Had Russell's head been turned by one of the wealthy backers, or by Jeffries himself, he considered. Either way this needed resolving.

"Back in a sec." he left Armstrong standing with half a prawn mayo triangle handing out of his mouth.

Jeffries had taken a call just as Steve stepped away, so hadn't noticed his boss heading towards him. Before he reached him, the older man was out of the door in a hurry.

"All alright?" Came the glamorous voice to his right.

"JT, lovely, good weekend?" Steve conceded he had lost Mark Jeffries for now, as his eyes trailed him out of the room.

"Are you sure?" her eyes joined his watching the door close. "Is he alright today? Seems a bit off colour?"

"Not sure myself, I am a bit concerned about him." He turned to face JT. "We cleared the air last week, but he's been a bit, well, a bit off this morning. Can't put my finger on it."

"It's a great trait Steve. You two may not get on like peas in a pod, but yet his wellbeing is important to you. Very admirable, my love." with that, she cast herself off into the room like an apparition.

It was some moments later that Russell beckoned everyone back to their seats for the continuation of the meeting. The murmuring subsided, replaced by the clink of china plates stacking, and chairs scraping back into place on the laminate floor. All seats were filled again, with the exception of one.

Just as Russell was about to raise his voice to question his whereabouts, Mark Jeffries returned to the room. The rosy, blotchy complexion of yesterday was back, along with a slight beading of sweat on his upper left brow, and lip line. A moment of frantic non-verbal interaction took place. JT eyeing Steve, everyone else eyeing Mark, and then John. Everyone looking for a reaction, or story.

"Right, what's next?" Russell began, looking down, clearly logging everything in his mind.

"Supplier arrangements." Mark crackled, taking a sip of water to steady himself.

Doing everything to avoid Steve's intensifying stare. His eyes powering down on Jeffries like the hail now beating against the large door at the back of the room. Creating an almost ritualistic, frantic, snared beat, which matched that of the Trading Director's chest as he strived to continue.

"I, I'm not, too sure we looked, I mean, we covered all the discussion last week." he struggled to begin.

Adrenaline pounding through his system clearly effecting his enunciation, until it had somewhat slurred.

Eyes flickered between the pair. All except JT, who remained firmly focused on Steve, forcing her eyebrows, and in turn her pupils, to convey her mix of discomfort and mild concern.

"I've asked Mark to bring this back up this week." John Russell commanded across the room, as if to stop fluttering eyes "Now, share with everyone, what you shared with me Friday night."

"Thanks John." Jeffries took a long breath, and more water.

"I've spoken to Kingsland again in the morning, this morning, and they can give us another percent on the margin. This. Er. Corrects the figures to the slide, to the ones on the slide here."

A slide appeared on the screen, which Steve had never seen. His blood boiled. Rage grew through his shoulders, into his neck muscles until it resided firmly in his molars which now clenched themselves together whilst he took a sharp intake of air through his nose.

The offer from Kingsland, the country's second largest supermarket chain was now really compelling. Steve could not fathom how he had pulled this off. The margin shift was massive, they were prepared to take millions off the price of the products they would sell them wholesale. This in turn would be worth millions in profit to Russell's over the coming years. The slide, a basic line graph, headed by large red font stating 'Private and Confidential' showed the difference it would make.

"So, this then gives us a three and five year projection." gaining control and balance, Jeffries clicked the slides forward.

As expected, this gave an almost ten million pound shift in profit by year three of the business plan. This was going to be hard to argue away, Steve reflected, as he spotted that the Company Secretary was hammering away the notes into her iPad. He glanced to Russell, who was, for once, captivated by the numbers. His ageing brain had still managed to work this forward to the resulting share price. The kudos of Kingsland a major factor, alongside the commercial terms, this now seemed like a no brainer.

"Excellent stuff Mark, just excellent!" he exclaimed. Jeffries allowed himself a wry smile in glance at Steve. Russell's attention turned to him also. "Not sure the rejections from last week hold much water now."

"They, er, want to keep this under wraps for now, it's understandably sensitive for them." The Trading Director leapt in, stealing the spot from his boss, and seeing a chance to land one more swinging boot to his argument "but this is watertight, they need us as much as we, well we really need them"

It was clear they needed better products. Other small retail stores had powered ahead with getting better quality food in stock. The current wholesale deal with The Wholesale Group (or TWG) was running behind the times. Retailers, both large chain and independent corner shops were running to the hills. The fruit and veg was average, and many of the ready meals looked like reconstituted dog food. However, right now, Steve needed to protect their deal. He was in deep, and now needed to swim harder than ever.

"Steve, your views? Russell the only one to break the tense silence in the room. It had only lasted a couple of seconds but had felt like an age.

"Clearly a good improvement." he couldn't bring himself to swallow a compliment aimed directly at Jeffries, so this would suffice "however, two significant hurdles for me."

Jeffries, still facing the projector screen, noticeably winced. Whether in frustration, resentment or fear, it was unclear. Quite possibly a mixture of all. Steve now leaned into the table, putting down his Mont Blanc, and rooting his elbows into the wood. Hands clasped together as if in prayer. Subconsciously, sensing something in the air, the others in the room sat back in their plush leather. Diverting their gazes to the screen or their notepads.

"One." he jabbed his left index finger in the air.

Tucking his right fist into his opposite elbow, naturally pushing him further into the table.

"Their length of terms is only 12 months, they are fronting none of the cost to switch out of the TWG depots, and who's to say that they won't bump their wholesale price day one next year? In full knowledge they have us by the bollocks."

He hadn't mean to swear, a mix of desperation, blended with a desperate drive to seize back the agenda item. This was the weaker of his arguments. He let it sink in, and gauged the reaction of the room.

There was enough sway. Enough tilts of heads, scrunching of faces in reluctant acceptance.

"And two," like a boxer going for the uppercut blow, "their delivery schedules are completely incompatible with our business."

Knowing he had used this argument previously, he had to avoid sounding repetitive. He had clearly not pushed them to improve this, and so, had had no contact with them to do so. This risk he took, knowing it was the more compelling issue for their business. Combined with the hail increasing its tapping on the door, and a distant rumble of thunder kept the atmosphere alive.

"They only deliver three or four days a week, and all bunched up. This just doesn't work. As most of you know," swaying his arms in attempt at including his peers, eyeballing each of them "TWG give us five days in small shops and six in big ones."

"Totally. This totally undoes all the great work my team have done with staff working patterns." Martin chipping in unprompted would add great value "The costs involved in moving would make some considerable dent in that."

Pointing at the projected profit improvements. He had made a great point. Steve refrained from acknowledging this in any form, so to disperse any argument of collusion from the men at three and nine on the circular table.

"Has that been factored in Mark?" Phil Bolton chimed in for unexpected support "I don't see any costs for alteration of IT system either. How are we expecting to plug into their forecasting algorithms? I'm not running an ethernet cable over to Swansea Mark."

A wonderful point from the IT man, oddly missed in Steve's planning, and one avoided last week. An out of the blue compound of support. Covering him well in this odd paradigm of blocking what was objectively best for the company. Given a few hard pressed negotiations, and especially given what Steve knew about the future of TWG.

Others chirped various, lightweight, positive and negative viewpoints to colour the debate, and save face in front of the boss. At which point, resignation swept over the Trading Director's face. He tried to hide it, but the screwed lip and raised right cheek fooled few. His updated terms should have swept consensus. He puffed his cheeks and took yet more water.

"I still like it." John Russell shook the room into silence, much as the clap of thunder had moments earlier. "Plenty to iron out but it feels right."

The old man loved to operate in this realm, a typical Myers Briggs ENFP. He felt his opinions.

"Steve. I'd like you to pick this up." ignoring entirely his previous vocal objections.

"Sure." Steve nodded, avoiding eye contact, but sensing Mark Jeffries almost choking on his water in the corner.

The rest of the meeting was lost in the fog of red that now stung Steve's eyes. He had seen Martin Armstrong's eyebrows almost hit the ceiling at the suggestion of Steve now leading the charge to resolve the bumps in the road, allowing a smoother proposal for Kingsland to be signed off by the people now flurrying away their equipment, in a dash to escape the room.

First to escape, was Mark Jeffries, who had his generic laptop bag on his shoulder before Russell had uttered a word, in asking if there was any other business. As much as Steve would like to give chase, through the company corridors and down him like a weak gazelle, this would arise too much suspicion. It would certainly not endear him to the ginger haired man now exiting the room, patting him firmly on one shoulder in silent recognition of what he had asked him to do.

"Boss?" Came the keen young voice behind him. Instantly recognisable as his young protege.

"Not now, I'll give you a shout later." Steve dismissed, and headed out.

The younger man had never seen his boss like this in a number of years working together. Granted he had seen the pressure on him increasing over that time, and the new role title came with a large dose of shoulder weight. This time was different however, and he could not put his finger on why.

Steve slammed shut the door to his office, more dust fell from the ceiling, and the closed window rattled in its frame. He tore his iPad out of his bag, flipping its cover numerous times in order to get the keyboard to stand. Just then, he raised it in his right hand, and launched it across the room towards the door still settling in its hinges. The complete lack of aerodynamics in the Apple tablet saw it flunk flatly to the floor only eight feet away, avoiding contact with all walls and furniture.

"Fucking piece of shit." Steve stormed.

Throwing his torso back into his large leather executive chair with such force that one of the metal feet, and plastic caster, raised off the floor. He flung his arms into the warm air above his head like an olympic diver, diving backwards off the highest board, before returning them to the back of his head. Interlocking his fingers as he did so, and staring blankly to the Artexed ceiling above. His eyes closed.

The shockwave seemed to clear space around his secluded room, there was no knock, no checking in from anyone around. The silence that follows such an explosion. The hail gently rattled his window, subsiding, like the storm in his head. Deep breathing techniques deployed, he worked slowly through the rage. Eventually, bringing his eye line back to the horizon. He could see the way forward.

Hands resting back on the desk, turning his chair towards the large windows that made the corner of this grand office space. He stared through the persistent drip from the ornate awning above, resolving to follow this through.

He lent over the side of his desk. Grabbing the bag that had served him so well for so many years. The middle section already open, he reached in, and unzipped a modestly hidden padded pocket at the bottom. Pulling out an older model iPhone.

Constantly on silent. Rarely used. He lit the screen with a press. There were no messages, no missed calls. This was rarely how it worked. He tapped out a message.

Issue. Back in review. Will need to lift lid.

Hearing a noise at the door, he hurriedly took the phone and tucked it under his thigh. Nobody entered. He checked the device.

1 message received.

He opened it, checking the door once more.

Not ideal, but understand.

This was the green light he needed. Gathering up his strewn tablet from the floor, and bundling it into his bag, he grabbed his suit jacket from the back of his door and exited.

Jacket on, and bag over shoulder, he peered his head around the small room a few feet away. Miles away, in a cacophony of the latest grime music, Charlotte sat. Steve tapped the wall, making her jump as she did.

"Sorry, sorry." she stumbled, pausing Stormzy mid spit. "The thunder was doing my head in."

"I'm popping out to get lunch." and with that he left.

Not waiting for the response. Certainly ignoring the dry sandwiches consumed only moments earlier.

4

He jumped into his car. For once, chucking the black leather bag in the front seat. Swinging the front out, narrowly missing the bumper of the Defender in front. He clicked his seatbelt into place after punching in his code for the flimsy barrier.

Foot down, he pushed away from the gate, and down the country lane. Seeing his own office in the rear mirror, he pushed a little harder on the accelerator. The V8 responded as it should, jarring him into the soft leather, until the building was out of sight.

The road eventually took him to a small hamlet on the outskirts of Ware. He pulled into the car park of the crumbling local pub. Tired and old, a manifested embodiment of its clientele. The bumpy, uneven gravel land played havoc with the suspension. He eventually bought the vehicle to a stop, ignition still running, in the corner next to a tangled metal storage unit, and a few aged kegs.

He searched in his bag for the zipped compartment, pulling out his phone and dialling the three number he needed.

"James, Can you talk?" The fact the other person answered alone should have told him the answer.

"Two secs, let me just move through here." whispered excuses could be heard, followed by flurrying footsteps, and a clicked closure of a door. "Right, fine, shoot."

Steve regaled all the details of the morning's meeting to the man on the other end. It was not the statistics, or profit projections that he needed to know. Only the change in stance.

"It needs to be in his name, and give it a few days to breathe." Steve concluded.

"Absolutely." the scurry of pen on paper heard clearly down the line. "I'm going to assume you've told…"

"Yes" Steve resolutely shut off the conversation.

"Good, good thing, OK." more scribbling "Leave it with me. Today's the 2nd, so I'll want to go for the 6th."

"Agreed, perfect." Steve sighed in relief.

He jumped as his other phone buzzed, and a loud ringing came from the car speakers. Charlotte calling him. He'd only been gone just over half an hour, but too long to just be grabbing a sandwich. He diverted it.

"Everything OK?" The man on the other line with a sense of jitters.

"Yeah fine, not to worry. Look, James, thanks." He calmed

"All in this together eh?" He replied, and hung up.

Steve took a moment to compose himself. Realising this was getting more intense. He longed to go into the pub and neck a quick pint before returning, but that was just not behaviour befitting his title. His eyebrow raised, and a wry smile came over his face. Clicking the automatic gearbox into reverse, he span around in the loose gravel, his indicator clicking him back onto the main road towards to the office. He dialled Charlotte's desk phone from his car as he drove. Straight to voicemail.

"Massive fucking queue, on my way back. Forgot about the two o'clock. Won't be long."

Arriving back in the office car park, he tucked in neatly behind Russell's machine and stepped confidently back into the building. Calm, and almost cheerful, a long way from his emotional state only an hour earlier. Only 5 minutes late for his next meeting, he had got away with a short lunchtime spin.

He opened his office door and to some surprise was met by three people sat around his table.

"Sorry boss, I thought we could sit in here when they arrived." gesturing to the other two. "Where's your lunch?"

"Ate it on the drive back." Steve bluffed "I was still starving after board!"

The others in the room chuckled with him.

"This is Rachel, and you already know Nathan from Office Diamonds." she explained.

Rachel was his new PA, due to be replacing Charlotte at the end of the week. Here for her first day introduction to how things worked. Steve could not believe his luck. The luck of the draw. She was stunning.

Small, petite, mid-20s, with long flowing blonde wavy hair. She reminded him very much of Margot Robbie from her role in Wolf of Wall Street, his favourite scene played out in his mind immediately, and almost missed the courteous handshake with both.

"Great candidate for you Steve." the over confident Nathan dived in "She's got a great CV, as you've seen, that's why I wanted to come down personally and introduce you. We are excited to have Rach on our books, as I'm sure you will be. I can see her fitting in well here."

The man had an ability to use fifty words, when five were sufficient. He also had a massively over-inflated sense of importance for a regional representative of East Anglia's number 2 recruitment firm. Today was stretching Steve's regularly thin patience for him. Clearly also wanting to make a good impression on young Rachel.

Her large, crystal blue eyes lit up as she turned to face Steve. The first time he had really seen them. Christ, he wished he hadn't. Mesmerising pools of azure. His composure was certainly malfunctioning today. She smiled, her imperfect smile only added to her appearance, a slight protruding tooth, hardly noticeable, but she wore it with pride.

"She's coming in.." Clearly realising he had started a sentence he couldn't finish. The rep looked at Charlotte for help.

"Thursday and Friday." she confirmed, a wry smile at Steve.

"Yep, that's it, Thursday and Friday. Blimey, where's the week going?" he babbled.

"So I think Charlie is going to show you round now." he turned to face the stunning blonde.

With that, Charlotte and Rachel commenced their own tour of the building. Whilst Steve did his upmost to dispose of the nauseating mess in front of him.

Once dispatched back to his company branded Hyundai i10, Steve reached into his bag to check on the flighted iPad. Surprisingly in decent enough shape, and this time he managed to manhandle the stand at the first attempt.

It was abnormal for him to have not checked the stock price already, as much a daily routine as his Caramel Macchiato. Clearly the stormy morning throwing him off course, so now was as good a time as any to review their goings on. Surprisingly, he saw the company was pulling out of its nose dive of Friday. Things were gradually edging up through the morning trade. Skipping through to the dealings, it was low to medium sized trades. Nothing significant, purely speculators seeing an opportunity. The chat rooms and forums were the key place for this info. Steve quickly flicked over to his favoured sites, which confirmed his hunch.

Various comments, surprisingly over the weekend, had referenced 'large supply deal', 'ground breaking supply change' or 'Supply changes afoot'. Steve sat forward, breathing through his hands as he processed the impact of this. Clearly info was seeping from this team, or were those at Kingsland were a bit loose lipped, neither of which tied up with Mark's approach earlier. Sometimes these things genuinely slipped out, discussions after work in the local bar, or friends of friends, a snippet of info used to leverage a couple of thousand at best.

Right now, this seemed no different. Nothing untoward causing it to buck the trend. He dusted the front of his blue Tom Ford two piece. Opening the small pack of mints he kept in his breast pocket.

Good timing, as Charlotte and Rachel returned from their whirlwind tour of the building. The giggling as they approached the door, negated the need for a knock once they got there.

"Yup!" Steve beckoned on the first sound of fist on oak.

The giggling continued slightly as the young women entered.

"Sorry, Steve!" Charlotte apologised, through a massive grin.

"Don't normally see people that happy around here." he quipped. Aiming to come across more light hearted than ever.

"Oh the boys in IT didn't know what hit them when I introduced Rachel!" the present PA chuckled. Her informality growing by the hour as her exit grew closer.

"Not surprised." Steve nonchalantly threw back, before catching himself "Not many people go to the cow shed."

The two women glinted an eye at each other. He had been rumbled, despite his scramble for professionalism.

"Grab a seat, I'll be with you in a second" he was on the path now, so should really continue. He tapped aimlessly at his iPad.

"I've got my meeting with HR." Charlotte reminded him.

"Oh right, yeah." his raised his head, hands clasped in front of him on the desk, turning his wedding ring with his right thumb and forefinger. "Grab a seat then Rachel. I won't be a sec."

What was he doing? He felt prickles in his cheeks, were they blushing? Was it warm in here?

The petite woman pulled out the chair from the middle of the table, smiled at her compatriot as she left, and began looking around the room. Taking it all in. Steve caught it all from the corner of his eye, hoping to regain some composure by scrolling through sales figures that he already knew. He took a deep, nasal, breath.

"Water?" As he grabbed a bottle from his small but noisy fridge.

"Er, no, thanks." a little shyness crept in.

He stood, and pulled up a seat next to her, and sat. Crossing his left leg on top of the opposite knee. Her disarming stare catching him, she smiled kindly and warmly.

"So, tell me about yourself." a lame, chat up line, normally reserved for the local bar. "experience? Education? All that jazz."

All that jazz? You idiot. Internally kicking himself in the stomach for good measure. Her smile returning from where it came, as she clicked into interview mode. Reeling off her educational background, and CV to date. A well educated, top half of the class student. Obviously some smarts to go with her looks. Steve listened intently, taking it all in, registering every word.

"Now I just live at home with my Mum." she finished. The prickles spread to the corner of his mouth, causing them to move upwards, as he relaxed back into his seat, hands hooked over his knee.

"Well it's great to have you." his voice dropping ever so slightly "so, come on, what's she told you?"

She giggled, a light joyous giggle, certainly not heard in these walls very often. Pushing her golden waves behind her ear, and looking straight at Steve.

"Oh a few things." she smiled again, a playful glint in her eye. "how to make coffee, and when to put my headphones in."

Charlotte was catching on quicker to how Steve worked than he had realised. Clearly not missing his outrage of earlier.

Rachel's approach, on the other hand, was disarming. Honest, but playful. He was on the back foot for the rest of their time together, as they covered more than just office logistics. Steve explaining how he liked to work, even admitting his occasional flare up. Failing to once discuss his spouse, despite further turning of the ring on his finger.

"Christmas party." He remembered out of nowhere, almost excited to tell her. "now that's a good one. We do a good party. Need to make sure Mags sorts you out."

She smiled, and looked at her hands.

"Well, I er, think that's probably about it." Steve realising he had dropped his guard too far, too soon "I need to go see someone."

"Of course." the cute blonde returned, with further movement of her hair "I'll go wait for Charlotte next door."

They parted. Steve heading straight to the gent's facilities half way down the corridor. Taking a cubicle to gather his thoughts. Hearing the door open and close a few times, his colleagues in and out in a few seconds, he took the time to pause. He realised he needed to get control on the one emotion he had never had much success with.

Needing to deal with a few misfiring chemicals in his brain, he resolved to get back to what he knew best, work. He needed to clear a few things up, and get the foundations laid ahead of the end of week earthquake he had just set in motion.

The brisk walk there had done much to clear his mind. Fresh air, even warm and stuffy air like today, did wonders for him, it always had. Opening the door to the IT department, he was met with a waft of cool circulated air, and as low, melodic whir of fans driving that air into the circuits of the many computer units evenly spaced out on the white desks.

Nobody was sat at these desks. Instead they were all stood towards the right hand side of the room, surrounding three large dry-wipe white boards. In front of those boards, vigorously affirming an instruction was Bolton. The Scot loving a daily and weekly team huddle, a chance to broadcast to his citizens, in their tiny seceded archipelago.

"Ohh and we have a special guest guys." the richness of his vowels still resonating his heritage. "many of you won't have met Steve Bellingham, our new COO."

Whilst this would have been considered a slight from anyone else, in Phil's world, they were not as exposed to Steve's commanding presence as those in the main block. He raised his arm as if on a royal carriage, and turned to acknowledge both sides of the gathering.

"Clearly needs me for something!" he jested, to a generous ripple of laughter. "so I think that's it for today guys, thanks again. Have a great week!"

With that, the gathering dissipated. Many silently back to their workstations, some heading back to the mainland for some sustenance. The newer air conditioning units dealt with the increased muggy air ,from the open door, with barely a flicker. Maybe Steve should move his office here as well, he wondered.

An acknowledging nod towards his office from Bolton told Steve all he needed to know. Also signalling Bolton knew exactly why he was here. The IT Director had done well in Steve's estimations today, fully justifying the focus he had put on this relationship in his early years.

"Need something to break, chap?" By fat the most casual Phil had been with him.

"I mean! Fucking hell!" Steve retorted.

"What was the man playing at? I weren't gonna leave you guys stranded there, not after last week." No surprises that Bolton saw himself on some World War II, United States-esque saviour mission.

"Really appreciate it Phil, you know that."

"You know my position Steve, the deal will be good for the business, but bad for my team." which did not need translating to read it would be bad for Bolton, and the future of his job.

"They'll be gone in a year, less, I just can't do it to them Steve, I can't. But I can't obviously say that in there."

In many ways, he was right, the Kingsland deal would mean a significant drop in headcount in his team. Once the systems were in sync, there was little to no need for at least half of the studious, young, individuals sat outside. Clearly, Bolton took that as a personal affront, but also fearing for his own position, fully aware a smaller remit may revisit the Directors' position.

"Their systems are shit as well, Steve," he continued

"I could tell you all about their GDPR risks." well aware he would not need to.

"When have I let you down Phil?" Steve charmed, the perfect dose of subservience and trust building.

"Ha! Now that's fair." the man twisted his mouth in agreement "bit more power too now! Eh, chap?"

"Well, look, I just wanted to pop over and thank you for the support in there. You get it, and I know you're on the same page."

"Of course Steve, got your back."

"Cheers Phil, never doubted it." Steve moved to leave the room, shaking the Scotsman's hand in appreciation.

As he left through the opened panel door, he turned, leaning through the closing gap, shoulder on the frame. "Might need a favour later in the week."

"Why doesn't that surprised me?" he chuckled. Sending a thumbs up to the COO as he watched him leave.

Walking back past the banks of desks, the rhythmic combination of keyboard tapping and rain dripping on the skylight the only other noises above the mechanical hum, he exited into the stuffy car park. Hurriedly stepping as the light drizzle suddenly intensified, making it to the reception entrance awning just as the downpour began hammering down once more. Steve stopped under the refuge, looking into the clouds, breathing long and deep, soaking in the freshness. Almost as if it gave him a renewed sense of energy and deepened his reserve for what was coming next.

As the thunder rumbled again, a couple of miles away, he took himself back into the company building. Catching sight of the scuffed black department store brogues of Mark Jeffries as he disappeared to the floor above. Give him a minute, Steve resolved. Taking a cup, and pouring some water from the nearby cooler. He looked out the window as if to review the status of the storm. Smiling as he did so.

Scrunching the thin plastic cup, and throwing it firmly into the small grey bin next to him, he glanced briefly at the copies of British Retailer sat on the low table. Just as it would be on tables around the country, at any other retail company office reception area. The real news came via their website, especially in a fast moving industry such as this, but the print still had its place. He grabbed the latest copy, rolling it in his hand and heading up the stairs after Jeffries.

By the time he reached the second floor, Jeffries was tucked away back in his office. Steve already knew his plan, but his sadistic side needed exercising. He had been spotted on the department already, his colleague deciding to side eye him on entry and continue feverishly tapping away on his desktop.

Steve strolled the floor, small localised greetings to the different sub teams. All perched from the corner of a desk within sight of the slender office. These people didn't know of his distaste for small talk, or at least they didn't let on, and engaged vigorously in discussions ranging from football to the latest reality show. Steve just soaked it up, aware that Jeffries eyes were straining through the side of their sockets.

Akin to a killer whale playing with its prey before the fatal act. He enjoyed this once in a while. Working with Mark for a number of years, he knew his anxious foibles inside and out. Granted, he had caught Steve off guard earlier in the day. The mature seal managing a small nip of the whale's fin, barely noticeable after a while, and one that would cause the seal to have his own agonising inevitability dragged out just a little longer.

"You got a sec Steve?" Crackled confidence from the Trading Director now standing behind him.

"Always Mark, your place or mine?" He lightheartedly chuckled, playing to the wider audience, who responded in light sniggers.

"Mine if that's alright?" He stumbled, unable to muster an ability for banter at this time.

Steve closed the door, casting an exaggerated wink to the group they had just left, which met with a small chortles as they continued their work. The two men resumed their normal positions once in the office, one defended behind his fabricated desk, hiding his shaking right hand, whilst one perched nonchalantly on the corner of the table. Steve now regaining the upper hand in all senses, despite the less than neutral venue.

"Look, Steve." Mark mustered "about.."

"Mark." Steve interjected "seriously, stop panicking, I'm not here for blood."

"But…" a confused feeling swept over the older man.

"Of course I'd rather you bought it to me than going straight to Russell." calmed Steve. Relaxed, outstretched hands matching his slightly shrugged shoulders.

"I was going to, but it was all so quick." Mark tripped and stumbled through his lie. "And after Friday, well, yeah."

"That's what I guessed." he paused "Next time, just drop me a text, or pick up the phone."

The reaction on Jeffries' face was a priceless picture. Lost for words, colour drained, and jaw ever so slightly hanging.

"I'm out in shops tomorrow with Martin. Need anything looking at?" Steve pivoted.

Mark had little response, caught desperately off guard. The hand shaking had subsided, but only to transfer to his heels which now bounced vigorously under the desk, as adrenaline seeped from his body. Preparation for the fight, or flight, that never came, he had been disarmed, and now suffering in his chemical crash. He sipped the last of his mug of water.

There was no handshake, Steve could only bring himself to so many pleasantries. He stood, leaving the unravelled magazine on the table behind him, phone already in hand, desperate to deploy the play some more with his puzzled prey.

Leaving the office, treading confidently over the shabby blue carpet squares, he waited until the department door had clicked closed behind him, and punched his security code into the keypad on his phone.

To: Alison

Need your expertise, pop up ASAP. S

5

"The next piece we need to talk about this morning are the continued troubles at TWG. For those of you not working in the food or retail sector, these guys are, or at least used to be, one of the biggest food wholesalers in the U.K. with over ten thousand employees across the country."

"Yeah that's right Mikey, recently things haven't been so good for them though. The entry of the big 4 supermarkets into wholesaling has completely changed the landscape. Customers can now go pretty much anywhere and get the branded food they know and love, even in their local corner shop."

"Even bigger convenience store chains have been moving away from TWG now."

"Totally Mikey, only a few weeks ago PriceCutter announced they were cutting. That they were cutting ties with TWG. It's also being rumoured now that

Russell's are getting into bed with Kingsland. Both companies saw a real spike in their share price yesterday, on the back of rumours over the weekend."

"I can see it happening, Izzy, both sides are keeping very quiet at the moment, but there's no smoke without fire. Russell's just can't continue with TWG, I don't know if you've tried their food recently, but its like the leftovers in a bargain bin."

"Can't say I have Mikey!"

"Well a single man needs to eat, and can't be too picky after a 3am start! The point I'm making is that they just aren't as good as the shop a hundred meters further down the road where our studio is based. They are getting left behind the other players in the market, and I would say they need to move on this deal quickly."

"Pretty much the death knell for TWG though, losing one of, if not their biggest, customer."

"The price of not moving with the times, Izz. You're right, they will struggle to hold much ground after that, and I can't see beyond some widespread redundancies there. They've just been squeezed out in, what is now, a very competitive market. Well I'm sure we will pick up more on this as the morning goes on, but right now its six thirty, and time to go over to Bhavina with the news."

Steve listened to Money Matters almost every morning. A daily dose of what was happening across business sectors, but rarely was it so close to home. The continued share price spike of yesterday was a self fanning flame, rumour driving rumour, that threatened to derail his plan. Overnight, anxious texts had been received on the phone now zipped safely away in the bottom of his carry bag.

The early morning, long drive, from Northampton to Widnes was exactly what Steve had needed. Martin had been only too pleased to accept a day visiting various shops around the area, and it had only needed a few low level meeting cancellations, a rare quiet day in the diary of the new COO. Two thirds of the way into his three hour trip, he pulled into the Starbucks drive thru just off the M6 for his regular morning tipple.

Order placed, he waited in the queue behind a sleek Porsche Cayenne, and checked his phone. An abnormally early meeting request from John Russell, not even via his own PA, for Friday afternoon. Steve smiled to himself, the old man was clearly seeing pound signs in his eyes as he stared at the Kingsland rumour fire. He accepted without hesitation, knowing deep down, that meeting would not be happening.

"Cheers pal." he grinned widely at the sombre-looking server.

Driving away, contemplating how this week was going to be the start of the end for the older man. The countdown clock that had been ticking away for a couple of years, had now begun to speed up ever so slightly.

He arrived ahead of schedule, pulling his sleek, sparkling clean Jaguar around the side of a run of terraced houses. Turning again, down the narrow alleyway, passing dented garage doors, flaking off various colours of paint. Tagged by various spray cans over the years, he passed uncollected large, red, wheeled bins, with their bags spilling out from under the weighted lids. The alley opening up to a small unmarked car park, pulling himself over the uneven surface and up to the curb, with a slight bump.

Looking around, the shop front was just off to his right, the end of a four shop parade. One of the metal shutters had failed to retract itself completely into the roller, and was now left hanging at an angle.

Running down the side of the building was a rickety grey fence, overgrown weeds peeking through the gaps, desperate to escape, he thought. Above the ageing shop front, was clearly a residential property, cracked wooden windows, with mottled paint, opened, exposing off-white net curtains that now fluttered in the light breeze.

The overflowing of bins was not exclusive of the properties to his left, as he noted the chip papers and kebab carriers from the takeaway next door making their jump from the council provided waste facility. Nobody cared for this place. As he sat in his car, fully aware that this likely cost more than most of the properties in the area, he sipped his expensive coffee and turned off the engine.

He had lived a relatively privileged life, never wanting for anything, and so he could never have imagined living here. A scene replicated across northern England, suburbs of the smaller cities, cut off from the blood flow of London and the south east. Raised on the affluent part of the south coast, the views in front of him now would have seemed alien to him as a child. Yet, looking upon the child being manhandled into the shop, riding in his basic pushchair, by a mother barely 18 years old, he considered that they only knew this as their normal. Sipping his coffee, watching, contemplating, if the child was happy.

As they left the unit, he established that the child clearly was happy. Grinning ear to ear, sat in his miniature knock-off Liverpool shirt, and drinking from his freshly purchased bottle of Diet Coke. Steve then watched as he pulled out a warm grey meat pastry and stuffed it into his little face. The happiness, however, quickly turned to tears as he dropped the bottle on the floor, drink spilling everywhere, and facing a stern foul-mouthed rebuke from his teenage mother.

So engrossed was he in this scene of family feud, he hardly noticed Martin pull his smart, blue, Volvo alongside him. Continuing to observe the resulting slap on the arm, and speedy exit from the scene. Bottle now only half full stuck firmly in the child's mouth, as they pushed around the side of the row of houses and disappeared around the back.

The loud tap on his window bought him back to the moment. Armstrong stood, besuited, ready to greet his leader.

"I know what you're gonna say." he greeted him.

"The shutter will be fixed today, I'm fuming already and it ain't even eight o'clock."

"Hear the radio on the way up?" Steve brushed off.

"Yeah, fucking MJ." he paused "Good for share price though, if nothing else, wish I'd bought some a while back."

The younger of the two trying a compatriot wink.

"Only kidding, of course!" he retracted at the unreciprocated action. "Insider trading and all that."

He sucked air through his teeth in an exaggerated moment of nervousness.

"You done?" Steve cut, but with a warm smile to diffuse the nerves "Right, tell me about this one."

Armstrong proceeded to roll into a well-prepared fact file on the shop they now wandered towards. The two of them eyeballing the building from different angles, as if buying a second hand car. Just shy of kicking the tyres, Steve kicked away the chip wrapper clamped to the top of his Ted Baker brogues.

"Manager's name is Rohit. Nice guy, got some smart ideas about the place."

Rohit, was as promised. Entertaining, and jovial, as he toured the two senior men around his empire. A broad Scouse accent interwoven with his native Indian tongue, as he occasionally shouted instructions at his staff.

Local customers, so similar to the earlier scene, flowed in and out of the shop. Crisps, fizzy drinks, and cheap chemical filled sweets, the menu for the morning in this part of the world. Nothing much changed through the later hours, as schoolchildren arrived for the same smorgasbord of sugar on the way to their lessons. What a state this country was going to be in over the coming years, Steve mused. That floppy haired chef on television had an uphill battle getting these meals right.

Nothing much changed in the next four stores the pair visited that day as they worked their way across the top of the Peak District, a mixture of rundown building work, broken refrigerators, and sullen staff. The last shop, therefore, was light relief. A well put together building, crisp and clean. The noticeable difference in the shopfront which had no litter, all the lights working and windows in tact. Martin proudly reaffirmed that this shop they had in fact, only recently purchased, from Kingsland. Irony lost on him, but not on Steve.

"Afternoon loves!" came the bright cheerful voice of Karen, the Manager from the doorway. Immediately signalling their arrival this side of the Yorkshire border "Got kettle on, fancy a brew?"

Steve loved this part of the world. The drive on the A628 a bit of a guilty pleasure. Slow and winding roads, today, made even slower by numerous tractors. The breathtaking scenery more than made up for it. Views over the rolling hills framing the beautiful Torside reservoir, were a far cry from the sights of the morning. Grey and drab metropolitan style towns slowly disappeared as they climbed higher into the hills. This made way for rich greens and blues, the air even seemed fresher, with Steve rolling down his window most of the way over after the sun had made an appearance. Only the most hardened, soulless, person would fail to find joy in such a place. Best of all, there was next to no phone signal, leaving him in peace to soak it in. All of which put him in a great mood for a brew with the bubbly blond now sat with him.

"Never got to see the big cheeses at Kingsland." she began "So it's lovely to have you chaps here."

"He likes the drive." Martin chuckled with a nod towards his boss.

The lighthearted chat continued until Karen briskly cut through. A brief, but honest question, she had clearly been holding back at the dam.

"So I hear we are getting bought by 'em!" flicking her head towards the large Kingsland logo still emblazoned on the canteen wall. "We only just escaped!"

"Don't believe everything you read." the COO delivered, ominously.

"It wasn't the best, stock not coming in, deliveries missing, lots of food one day, nothing another." She rattled off "Oh I didn't know if I was coming or going some days."

Karen raised her eyes to the sky, picturing the chaos that had been dropped on her store the previous Christmas.

"Betty and Flo aren't too keen on the veg." waving her arm to her generically named customer base, the two names representing a thousand older customers nearby. "but I'll tell ya, I'm not throwing away half as much."

Martin dived in with the statistics. Reeling off stock and sales figures, as if either of the two people with him were interested, or impressed. Neither was true. This needed the personal touch.

"On my word, it won't happen. I promise you, Karen." Steve looked her straight in her eyes, raising his branded mug in absence of a Champagne glass.

"I'll drink to that, love." Karen smiled as she chinked mugs.

They wandered round the store for a while, chatting to the regulars, all of which effused positivity about the lady stood nearby. Planted pleasantries or not, it left the gentlemen with a good feeling as they walked out to their respective cars to wrap up the days work.

"Boss?" Armstrong asked sheepishly as he turned to face Steve in the rear car park "You know she'll be on my arse if Kingsland goes through."

"It won't." resolute, Steve smiled.

"Russell seems convinced, how can you be so sure?" Clearly troubled, the younger man was rarely so challenging.

"Martin," placing his left hand on the man's right bicep. "when have I let you down?"

"Never boss, never." The hanging rhetoric question should really have been left.

"Seriously, best boss I've ever worked for, you know that. The things you've done for me."

Martin was always gushing. His downfall in many aspects, unwavering loyalty to the man who had given him tidbits from the big boy table over the last few years, and had now given him a seat at it. He was not aware he was just a knight in this game of chess. More power than the lowly pawns, but still pretty limited in his movements.

Breaking eye contact, Martin looked to the floor, before returning his gaze to Steve.

"I mean it Steve."

"I know. Decent day." Steve accepted grudgingly whilst moving on, trying to end the reverence. "Enjoyed it, lots to get your teeth into."

"Totally boss, and I won't let you down. I'm on it." shaking his notepad full of Steves wishes through the day.

"I know." Steve returned.

The two men climbed back into their vehicles, engines started almost in tune. Steve sat back in his leather chair, and flicked the switch for the electric window to move down gracefully. Waving over at the man next to him to do the same, a slight squeak from the Volvo.

"Thinking about it, I might need a favour." Steve dangled.

"Anything, Steve, just ask. Need a bullet taking?"

"Not quite," he chuckled loudly, leaving Armstrong with a puff in his chest.

"Will let you know tomorrow."

With that, he reversed out of his space, and headed back towards the M1, and his waiting wife.

6

. . . .

The gentle rising piano of Einaudi's Nuvole Bianche woke him. Not that he had been deep asleep. He swiftly leapt to his feet and flicked the radio's switch, turning it off.

"Blimey you're up quick." Sarah grunted, still half asleep.

"Big day." he whispered, whilst stepping gentle out of their large bedroom "See you tonight."

Slowly, he edged the door closed, holding the handle so the latch wouldn't clunk shut. Knowing Sarah would nearly be back to sleep already, he stepped more meaningfully across the landing to his bathroom. Why they had one each, he never fathomed. Hers was a clean, well organised affair, never a toothpaste stain, or out of place bottle in sight. Steve's, however, was a sporadic collection of dark coloured bottles and sprays. A distinct manly odour filled the nostrils of anyone that entered.

This was the morning he had been waiting all week for, no surprise then, that he had hardly slept. Anticipation more than nerves, he considered as he brushed his teeth, flushing through with a sharp sting from the mouthwash.

He selected one of his favourite suits from the rail hanging in his home office. A sharp navy D&G number, well cut, despite its age, and his lack of chiseled features. It flattered him somewhat, just like a good suit should. A couple of sprays of his large bottle of Tom Ford, and he was ready. Somewhat bounding down the stairs, to collect his bag, and sweep the Jaguar keys off the side table.

"Good morning, it's Friday, it's five o'clock, and it's time for Money Matters with me, Mikey Russell."

"and me, Isobel Dacourt. Today's top money story…"

He flipped the paddles on his steering wheel, and turned the radio volume down, preferring to be alone in his head with his thoughts, and soon, his liquid breakfast, from the drive thru. He had pulled all the threads of his plan, over and over again, checking its strengths and weaknesses. It had been a rash, swift, move initially, but it seemed to stack up pretty well. His head would barely be above the parapet at any time, he had people to do that for him now.

An uneventful drive to the office was just as required, pulling up, coffee in cupholder earlier than most mornings, the clock barely passing six on the dial. He swiftly parked, and grabbed his items before heading inside. A cursory glance at the car park revealed that it was only him and a couple of keen Buyers at this time.

"Morning boss!" Colin cheerfully greeted him "Sorted that post problem for you."

"Cheers Col!" Steve chirped without breaking stride.

Sipping the coffee in his hand, he sat at his desk and pawed through his post, but also the couple of misdirected pieces that Colin had kindly placed with them. Smiling, he moved these to one side of his desk. The coffee had gone down an absolute treat, and as if by clockwork, it was now making its way swiftly through his system. He checked his watch just to confirm as much, and, leaving his door slightly open, he went to relieve himself.

Staring up to the top row of tiles, he took a deep breath. It was the only time of the day that this room didn't require some sort of breathing apparatus, right now wasn't far off, however. A heady mix of urinal cakes and cheap disinfectant stopped him mid-breath. He exhaled, finished, zipped up, and wandered back to his room.

The office door was closed as he approached. A small roll of his eyes, he should really be more specific. The rest had gone smoothly, clearly, as the post items he had left on the corner of the desk were now gone. He checked his watch once more, then sat comfortably back in his chair waiting for the ping of his iPad denoting a new email.

Moments later, slightly earlier than normal, there it was. The daily email that retailers around the country, digested with their breakfast.

British Retailer Exclusive - Russell's close to confirming Kingsland deal.

He grinned wider than he had for a while, and pressed firmly on the screen to open the mail.

Russell's Director leads supply transformation to Kingsland wholesale. British Retailer editor in chief James Radstock can reveal.

Mark Jeffries, Trading Director at Russell's, has been instrumental in pulling the deal together. Confirming this week their move to the supermarket giant's wholesale arm.

Read the full story here…

Steve gleefully perused the article, which was beautifully well written. Not quoting Mark, for obvious reasons, but enough to place the news directly from that horse's mouth. Sporadic snippets and statistics from the Monday meeting had been cleverly woven in, focused entirely on Jeffries being the one to lead the charge for the deal.

The editor in chief had even been cheeky enough to praise Steve's handling.

It's clear that new COO Steve Bellingham is keen for his team to take the limelight. Leaving Jeffries to be the man catching the golden goose.

He chuckled, before readying his game face. The next few hours were going to be his toughest since arriving here. Glancing at the time on his iPad, knowing Russell would be pulling into the car park anytime soon, and reading this very news story as he entered the building. God help anyone that got in his way this morning. Steve stood, ready to be that person.

Just as expected, Russell entered the building barely ten minutes later. Steve had been faffing around with a few less than important things near reception so he could spot his entry. His phone had rung silently in his pocket multiple times, more industry press, national financial papers, as well as a couple from his counterpart at Kingsland. The voicemails would not be pleasant to pick up, but this was the price to pay.

"My office! Now!" stormed Russell, as he burst through the reception doors. Mobile phone glued to his ear.

Steve kept silent, following the bright red glow of his senior. The freckles on Russell's face almost glowed like lights against the crimson red in his cheeks.

"Yep I'm with him now, call you back in ten." ending the call without waiting for the other side.

"Fuck!" He stormed, climbing the stairs.

Then, silence, like the moment before the storm, the two men walked awkwardly down the dim corridor towards Russell's vast suite. Almost half a floor of expanse space, the best view in the building by far. Ornate ceiling work and window frames immaculately painted, this was a haven.

He slammed his keys and phone down on his large wooden desk. A rich mahogany, matching that of the boardroom table, and that of every piece of furniture in this room alone. No cracked laminate in sight. The keys slid to a halt half way across, the phone bouncing to a stop in a similar position.

"Fuck!" He repeated. Hanging his suit jacket on the carved stand,   followed by some indecipherable mutterings.

"I can't believe him." Steve uttered.

"Fuck, fuck, fuck!" Russell seemed to be stuck in an expletive laden loop, some sort of vocational Tourettes.

He sat on the smart leather Chesterfield underneath the coat stand, nodding at Steve to join him on the matching chair opposite. Separated only by a small round marble topped table. Four chilled bottles of water stood, dripping with condensation, that made them look like they were sweating as much as their owner.

"We need to get him in here." Steve pushed to break the loop.

"No." Russell abruptly snapped through. Elbows on knees, he hunched forward, rubbing his fingers past his reddened forehead. "We need to think."

The collaborative statement pleased Steve, there was no need convince the fidgeting man opposite that this was not his crime, that his finger had not been on the trigger.

"You're right." Steve smartly conceded.

"I don't understand why!" Russell hadn't lifted his head. Confusion, frustration, and anger riddled the old mans mind. "Brian is fucking fuming. Wants to scrap the whole thing."

Brian Dickson was the man trying to reach Steve previously, and when he wasn't able, he had gone straight to Russell himself. No real sweat, either way this deal was dying. Steve remained silent.

"Fucking hell, Mark." shaking his head "We need to get a statement out, shut these bastards up." flinging one hand at his buzzing phone, before returning his fingers to his eye sockets, trying to scrub out what he had just read.

"I think patience is key." Steve calmly spoke "Maybe we can use it as leverage."

"He gave them details of the fucking deal Steve!" the bloodshot eyes now glared at him, like fiery rage "He told them the deal, and now Brian's got every fucking corner shop owner on his case wanting improved terms. It's not even 9 o.clock!"

Steve's heart was pounding in his chest. Adrenaline coursing through his veins. Excitement, anticipation, and a hint of nerves.

"That's for him to sort, not us." he countered. "He's the one screwing them to the wall."

A grunted acknowledgment from between Russell's hands. Not an agreeing one, but not dismissive. Slowly Steve continued to chip away. Until the phone buzzed again on the desk, this time Russell stood to look, as if a sixth sense had notified him to Jeffries' repeated calls over the last couple of minutes.

"He's here." Russell stated after picking up one of the three voicemails from the Trading Director. "I'll call him in."

Russell moved to return the call, Steve stood briskly.

"No." sternly stopping Russell from pressing the green call button, his thumb hanging, suspended above the screen. "Let's go to him."

The idea flashed behind the older man's eyes. He had no frame of reference, no precedent for this, and so, no grounds for disagreement. Had the retitled HR Director been in the room, she would have argued against a perceived ambush of his office. One of many reasons why Steve had planned this path. The two men sombrely headed down the corridor. Both engrossed in their phones, with not a word spoken. Messages sent to keep the various contacts in a holding pattern until they were able to be processed.

Only a handful of the trading floor team were in already. The Friday factor hit this part of the building more than most. Dress down day, also seemed to coincide with slightly tardier time keeping. Despite the mufti maxim, the two men approaching were of different ilk. Approaching, it was clear the lights were off. A muffled, frantic voice permeated through the thin wall. The content of the conversation was unclear, its tone, however, was as clear as crystal.

Eyes flicked over to the pair as they knocked on the door. Before scurrying back under their monitors, desperate to hear and see, but not be spotted. They had all read the article by now. They had all seen their leader enter the department in desperation, darting to his office without a word of greeting. The same beady eyes though, were not present to observe the earlier visitor to the room. A conduit for the mislaid post, that now sat casually on the table. Steve spotted it in an instant, as did Russell, but it was only of interest to the former.

Mark Jeffries was pacing along the window, the floor creaking under his heavy steps. Grey carpet tiles, loosened occasionally as he paced. Every sinew in his forearm straining to convey his words to the faceless caller. Aware of the two gentlemen sat at the table, he continued to verbally spar. Until he conceded.

"I understand." he resigned, ending the call, and taking a deep breath as he readied for his next battle.

"Grab a seat, Mark." Russell started.

"John, seriously, before you two start." he almost leapt back to his feet "This wasn't me."

"Then why is your name all over it Mark?" The older man restrained and controlled.

"I don't know, I don't know! Someone, somewhere!" waving his hand towards the trading floor. Eyes searching the ever more populated floor like a spotlight for his culprit.

When this culprit didn't appear he slumped into his seat. Head in hands.

"They want to call the deal off." he mumbled through his palms.

"I know Mark, I've already spoken to Brian." Russell delivered deadpan into the room, and let it hit each of them. "I don't know why you did it pal."

The softened approach, and genuinely sympathetic manner seemed to sooth Jeffries, who eased back and revealed his drained face, and ashen expression. The colour had long left, not helped by the grey blue hue across the room. Especially in the absence of the fluorescent glare. The only glares now came intermittently from the team outside the office door, blatantly slow walks past, hovering at nearby desks. All of which to put them in earshot of the morning's events.

"This wasn't me, John." softer, defences broken.

"I can't believe you, Mark, they've named you, the details you gave at board on Monday, it's there." Russell waved his hand at the monitor of Jeffries' computer.

"Check my phone records, John." desperation swept over him "Check my emails."

The thought came over him in an instant, grabbing his phone from his pocket frantically. Unlocking it at the second scrambled attempt, and in a fury of heavy breaths.

"Look, look!" he demanded, scrolling through his call lists, twisting the phone for the other men to see. Nothing conspicuous.

"Mark, seriously, you need to stop." Steve's tone deliberate, his words expectedly fell on deaf ears as he leapt to his feet, dashing to his desk chair, unlocking his screen.

John Russell sat and watched the freneticism of his colleague, nee friend. Flashbacks of the conference from years ago running through his mind. The time he had saved him, he felt, from a career ending destruction. He put a big, kindly, hand on Steve's arm to stop him intervening. Jeffries' flurried mouse clicks, continually forcing breath, leaning in and out of the screen, until he stopped. The storm subsided. A puzzled look crossed the face of the former Warrant Officer. Any remaining colour drained from his tired expression.

"I…." He whispered incredulously "I don't."

The old man now stood, walking over to him, putting his burly arm around Jeffries' shoulder and looked into the screen with him, concern washed over him.

"I don't understand." Mark uttered "I didn't."

His stomach churned. If he'd had anything in him, it would have lined the small bin next to him by now. Steve stepped over to join him, eyes scanning the space under the desk, as he moved around the right side of the desk, conscious of his manner, he mirrored the concern of the other two, as they all stared into the screen.

Sent: Tues 3rd August - 13:12

To: James Radstock

Message: We need to talk, got some great news for you. Give me a call, my personal number is below

"John, I didn't, this isn't...." His heavy breathing interspersing his desperate tone.

Steve stepped closer, leaning into the desk to read the email. As he did, his foot knocked the small lidded black plastic filing box, that was balanced uneasily on the foot of the desk. Emptying its contents over the floor.

"Shit! Sorry Mark." he quickly reacted.

The three men all peered under, as the items sprawled out. At first the muffled sound of paper, swiftly followed by the glug of liquid, combined with the chink of china on glass alerted them all. The half empty bottle of Glenmorangie, rolled to a stop. Mark's favoured mug stopped next to his shoe, a small drip of honey coloured liquid bled out onto the square of carpet.

Russell slowly bent to one knee, picking up the mug in his large hand. Standing, he raised it to his nose, if only to confirm to himself, the extent of the incrimination.

Jeffries awkwardly rolled his chair back against the wall behind him. His skin grey, corpse like, he had aged 20 years over the course of the morning. The bright white light of the full screen email accentuated the dark shadows building under his eyes.

"Fucking pick it up, Steve." Russell commanded, conscious of the meerkat like staff peeking above their desks outside.

Steve knelt, reaching under the desk, swept up the bottle, and placed it back in the box from which it had been evicted.

Jeffries just stared, eyes flicking between the mug, and the bottle. He stared vaguely at Steve as he was scurrying under the desk, gathering up the various printed emails and business cards, trying to get them back in the box, around the standing bottle. He watched as John Russell stepped back, returning his arm to his side, and then into his jacket pocket.

"JT, can you go to my office please." he spoke briefly before hanging up.

The three men stood in silence for a number of seconds, that felt to them all, like hours. Steve began pacing along the window, breaking the hesitancy for action.

"John, I just can't, it's not mine." Mark spiralled into denial "It's not my bottle, I didn't, I'm clean."

His voice began to raise, so much that both men turned to look at him wide eyed, desperate to give him dignity.

"Mark, let's go to my office eh?" The old man spoke softy "Less prying eyes."

Standing, gingerly, he made his way to join his long term colleague at the now opened door, Steve following supportively behind, collecting Mark's keys from the desk, and locking the office door behind them. Making their way silently along the long corridor towards the ornate office of the CEO, avoiding the stares that came from the people on the desks lining the walk, less restrained now.

"Sit yourself down"

Russell gently guiding him by the shoulder towards the broad leather armchair, before sitting opposite him. Steve pulled up two chairs from the meeting table, facing them in to create a small huddle around the marble table. The final chair now filled by the People Director, silently entering the room.

"OK, Mark, are you comfortable for me to bring Jane up to speed." Russell began, slowly and calmly. An unprecedented situation for him, but one that played extremely well to his style and engagement abilities.

A silent nod from behind his hands.

Russell calmly regaled the facts of the morning. Through the email, it's content, the date and time it had been sent, not a fact was missed. JT hardly flinched, just sat, thin glasses perched on her nose, no reactions crossed her face. Even as Russell revealed the half drunk bottle of scotch, barely a flicker, the consummate professional, someone who was very well versed in events such as this.

"It wasn't me Jane, I didn't do this, I just don't understand, the email, the bottle, I'm clean." anger boiled through him, his colour shifting through shades of grey, to deep mottled reds.

"I don't know how the bottle got there, I can't remember, I, oh fuck." he hung his head further into his hands, attempting to hide from the confusion and uncertainty. Doubting his own actions, questioning his own sanity.

"Mark, firstly, I want you to know, I am mostly concerned about you, I need you to take some deep breaths and talk to me." JT dropped her acronyms, took her glasses in one hand, leaning forward and placing her other on Mark's knee.

Tears began to well in the man's eyes.

Skilfully, Jane walked Mark through the compassion driven next steps, making sure at every point he was comfortable with what she was saying, and in turn, suggesting they do now. Steve sat, silently, but nodding gently at each suggestion, feigned concern and empathy with the confused, sobbing, man opposite.

Eventually, the group agreed that Jeffries would take some "time out of the business" as JT had carefully positioned it. Each of them knew he would never return, despite the message that would go out to their colleagues later that day, and the words spoken to the man himself.

Steve was asked to step out and contact Mark's wife to come to the office and take him home. He could not question the support, but not a pang of guilt crossed him. No knots tying up his stomach, or palpitating heart, caused by the career ending sentence he had just masterminded.

Completing his assignment, from the privacy of the rear gardens, he stepped back around the front of the building, swiping his card for entry back into reception. As he did, he passed his Head Of Operational Communications, Alison Maxwell. A closed eyed knowing nod, thrown deliberately in her direction. She understood, and passed him with just a polite greeting for appearances, which he reciprocated, neither diverting course as Steve returned to the makeshift counselling session being carried out in Russell's office.

"She'll be here in ten, Mark." patting the man on the shoulder, squeezing it gently. Before sitting, casting a grimly resigned look to JT, who smiled kindly and nodded.

"Thanks, Steve." he meekly replied "I don't know what to say to her. To you all, I'm so sorry."

Jeffries had covered up a further struggle with the booze only a couple of years ago, something he had not shared with anyone, other than his wife of 40 years. She had been the one to find him sat in his shed, slurring an argument with the radio, and hammering nails into his workbench rather than the chair he was meant to be fixing. To her, this summon to the office would be painful, but not shocking. Her initial thought had been of him lying prostrate in his office after a heart attack, so a wash of relief had helped land the request to drop everything.

She arrived at the back entrance as instructed, Steve whisking her up the building's rear staircase to Russell's office, only passing a small contingent of payroll employees who registered no interest in the pair.

"Moira's here." Steve announced as they entered.

Tears streamed down Jeffries face. His hands shaking uncontrollably as his wife took them into hers, kneeling by his side, trying to see the face hidden behind.

Steve pulled his chair over for her to sit more comfortably, an action greeted with a kind and warm smile. He suppressed the murmured pang of guilt that had made its way into his throat. Clearing it with a small cough, he stood behind JT's chair. She reached over her shoulder to place her hand on Steve's.

Mark took some time to pass the story on, interspersing it with desperate confusion, disbelief, and tumultuousness. Eventually, slumping into an apologetically, frail, shadow of his former self. Moira helped him gradually to his feet, he was weak, as if struck by fever or disease. Slowly, Steve and his wife supported him to her car, putting him in the passenger seat and closing the door on him. Jeffries closed his teary eyes and nodded at the man through the window, before mouthing thanks to him, and staring straight out at the ground ahead.

Moira thanked Steve more verbally, and the two agreed to talk in the coming days, as Steve requested regular updates on the man's condition. He waited, until the vehicle was started, and raised his hand so it was visible in her rear view mirror. Waiting patiently for her to exit through the barrier system, and turning left down the country lane. He took a deep breath before turning and heading back into the open door at the rear entrance. As he did, he glanced to his left, to see a face at the ground floor window, Alison Maxwell had witnessed the events of the last few moments. Alone in the small photocopying room, she looked at Steve and smiled.

Maxwell was a true careerist. The second, and likely staunchest, ally of Steve Bellingham within these four walls, not that anyone would ever know. Living with her partner Amanda, only two miles from the office, she had started work here within weeks of Steve's first promotion. Whilst she had applied for the position legitimately, going through various stages, with no hands on push from Steve, she had been tipped off for the position by her long time colleague. A managed, vacuous inhale of allegiant individuals to his top table.

She had proved her worth, especially in such a connected position. Talking to everyone, knowing everything. The office now revolved around her, even the positioning of her new office had been a conscious effort. Colin and Baz had been only too keen to get their hands dirty and knock two smaller rooms together, little did they know, or care, that this gave Maxwell full view over the key intersection of three departments. Nobody could come, go, or have conversation in the space without her being aware. She had always impressed Steve, but this had topped the lot.

Until this week.

Her meticulous planning had paid off. A co-ordinated effort, but primarily, the plaudits would lay with her. Initially, ensuring Steve would be visiting shops on Tuesday, the same day as timed email was set up at the crack of dawn from Mark Jeffries office PC, ready to leave his outbox at the correct time. Her hardest challenge had been getting the bottle into the office, but the carefully managed postal choreography of the morning had given her the desired cover.

It was the foresight to pour a small damning drop of alcohol into the mug that truly impressed Steve. He had to fight his pride as it slowly dripped onto the carpet, like blood at a murder scene. She had excelled herself, and would need to be rewarded in kind.

For now, they just acknowledged each other glances. Steve closed the door behind him, and stepped back up the stairs. Ready to draft the announcements that were going to rip millions out of the value of the company. As he reached the office door, he smiled.

7

"Now, this morning we are following on from yesterday's story, and the troubled times at wholesaler TWG." the soft morning voice of Izzy Dacourt emitting from the speakers.

"There are concerns the company will make an announcement today to close another of their distribution sites, putting a further 450 jobs at risk. They just don't seem to be pulling out of this nosedive."

"Well yes, you could say that Mikey. It's not looking good for them, really bad timing. Russell's share price seems to be getting hit hard on the back of it too, as pretty much the only major player still partnering with them."

"Bit of a rollercoaster few months for them, Iz, they were riding high after that article in British Retailer confirmed their move to Kingsland. Only to walk it back by the end of the day. That must have hurt all three businesses, but it seems only Russell's and TWG have shown the scars."

Rollercoaster, that didn't begin to describe it, Steve reflected, as he stopped at the traffic lights half a mile from the office. Sipping his coffee, he grinned, and a small snigger escaped through his nose, not for the first time he considered how well he had done out of the events now being broadcast on national radio. They were right, the share price had soared whilst they were holed up in Russell's office, topping out almost a pound a share higher than ever before.

Morality and ethics were tested in that short time, with each of the Directors sat around that marble table fully aware of the reality of the situation, the fragility of the mirage. Cashing out any shares at that point would have them hauled in front of the Financial Conduct Authority at a moments notice. Their team of highly trained experts had been monitoring every share deal, and those executing them, within hours.

Russell had gathered the other Directors in his room, informally, explaining the gravity of the situation. Eventually, refining the next steps, and readying them for execution. A well crafted internal announcement dispelled the myth about the Kingsland deal, which got the IT guys off the ceiling, and also served as an opportunity to address the Mark Jeffries situation. Whilst it was delivered with respect, and empathy, the departing murmurs and whispers proved that those being addressed had already joined the dots.

Once complete, a short statement was released to the press. Like piranhas fed for the first time in weeks, they tore it to shreds, dissecting every part of it for snippets of the real story. There had been no wiggle room to avoid dispelling the supply deal as pure hokum. However, Russell had been stalwart in ensuring Jeffries was given respect, finally settling on a concoction of poor judgment caused by stress, and illness, but an open admission of his grave error. This seemed to placate some, and temper the ferocity of the remainder.

Once out, the share price plummeted 60%, wiping millions of the value. Russell's personal fortune disappearing as the clock ticked on, until, eventually, trading was suspended. The old man had actually taken it well, more concerned for the wellbeing of those in and around the company. A strange byproduct of the events, he and Steve had become much closer. Strengthening their bond, Russell had latched harder onto Steve in the departing of his friend.

So much so, the old man now greeting him with a warm cheery slap on the back as they arrived in tandem at the front door of the building. Both men in early, ready for the conference call with TWG in less than 20 minutes.

"Good morning, Steven." his joviality surprising, given the circumstances, but was truly genuine. "another bashing on the radio on the way in!"

"Nothing new, John, any excuse to rake it back up." Steve replied, holding the door open.

"Very true pal, thank you, sir." he acknowledged in mock grandeur. "Anything I need to know for the call?"

"Nothing new overnight, they can't make Plymouth profitable anymore. Losing the South West Foods contract stuffed them up."

"Those bastards doing that a couple of weeks before Christmas, they knew the knock on." true concern on his face for the workers about to be laid off there in the next few hours.

"I think a few of them will get in at Bristol." Steve tried to offer as consolation.

"Good, good." the old man was still churning something "and you can't get Rich at South West to change his mind? You worked with him before?"

"Spoke to him last night, he needs to move over, so much competition down there."

The CEO's support for the current wholesale arrangements had come so far in recent weeks, that he was now rallying his network to support. Steve considered he may have done too good a job in convincing him a switch was a bad idea, especially as Russell's shares would take another hit today once

TWG released the official announcement, further punishment for his guided loyalty.

"Pop down just before the call if you can." another pat for Steve as he unlocked the door to his office.

Steve stepped inside and closed the door behind him. Nobody would disturb him for a few moments, especially as Rachel would not arrive until, at best, half past eight.

Instinctively, he checked the phone stashed away at the bottom of his soft leather bag. One message received.

How long? Time to set up a call?

He knew the context without needing to question. The total demise of TWG an important part of the plan, and timing here, as ever, was critical.

Yes, 3 weeks minimum, 4 weeks likely.

He fired off his response before deleting both messages, cursorily checking the room, and returning the phone to the bottom pocket of the bag.

Today was the precipice for the wholesale company, their finances would not be strong enough to see through the plan about to be communicated on the upcoming call. Considering his approach, the balance required, the nudging of those in the room, and those not, along this path. He gathered up his favourite notebook and pen in his right hand, glanced out of the window, inhaled his head up and shoulders back, and headed down to see Russell.

As he left his room, he poked his head around the door of the next office. Hopeful the light would be on, and Rachel would be there, setting up for her day. The dim greyness told him all he needed to know. He walked on, turning his wedding ring with his thumb.

"Grab a seat chap." Russell greeted warmly. "Tea? Coffee?"

"Nope, all good, had one on the way in." Steve sat around the larger of the two tables.

"You and that premium coffee! Never understood it myself."

Steve politely chuckled, a joke as old as time, almost a ritualised part of any morning summoning to this part of the building.

"Before the others come in Steve, I need to chat to you." the sparkle in his eyes descending into sombre solemnity, as he pulled a chair close to Steve, sat, staring at his hands for a moment.

"Everything OK, John?" Steve pushed the concern in his voice hard.

"Whew." he exhaled "Are you ever not sure how to say something you've been planning to say for a long time?"

"Yes." Steve lied "You're worrying me John."

"Steve, I've been thinking about the business. Everything. Mark, TWG, the investors." Russell's head lifted from his hand, and looked out of the full height elegant windows across the room. "And my age, I'm not getting any younger Steve."

Steve sat, soaking in the words. He was almost never referred to by his proper name, this was serious.

"Maybe it's time to make some plans," He continued "you know what I am saying?"

"I do, I disagree wholeheartedly." Steve argued.

"I thought you might." Russell chuckled, now looking straight at Steve. His bright green eyes bore through him. "I think it's time."

"Not now John. The waters are really fucking stormy right now." Steve countered. Russell loved a good analogy. "We need our Captain."

Chuckling, John Russell stood to his feet again, and stepped towards the window that had his eye for the last few moments.

"John, the timing is wrong." He pushed, the conversation had been inevitable for a while. "This is just a time for reflection, before we plot the next part of our course."

"Maybe you're right Steve, maybe you're wrong. I'm getting too old for some of this though. I'd like you to really think about what I've said. This stays between you and I, nobody else. They've got enough on their plates right now, and I'm sure the buffet hasn't stopped giving." slowly stepping away, returning his gaze to Steve.

"I agree, this next bit…" he was interrupted by a knock on the door.

Sporadically, the company Directors now gathered around the table, in the centre of which was an ageing speakerphone. The IT Director, last in, assumed his rightful place in setting up the call after a series of mumbled greetings to the rest of those gathered.

"Morning John." came the burly voice, crackling through the speaker. "Can you hear me OK? Who do we have on the line?"

"The whole board are here, Jack." Russell awkwardly looped his words aimlessly into the middle of the table, before smiling at his team, lingering particularly on the newest face in the room to give her a reassuring grin.

Jack Lewis, CEO of The Wholesale Group, began to outline their survival plan. As expected, the depot in Plymouth would close, and operations transferred to Bristol. Assurances were given about continuation of supply to the shops.

"Jack, we need more than words on that one. It's contractual and I, no we, expect you to honour that." Steve barbed. Whilst there was no deviance from the path they were on, he couldn't let this be seen as a cakewalk.

"Totally understand Steve, we have contingency in place at Bristol. Happy to memo that to your legal guys later. We know what we have to do."

A nod of appreciation from those physically in the room.

More details continued to spew from the speaker. White noise to Steve, but he kept a concentrated stare towards the middle of the table, whilst scanning his peripherals to gauge reactions in the room.

"Jack, Steve again, I just want to double back on that point about staffing in Bristol and Durham." Steve interjected as Lewis had dodged through an impending manpower issue. "Is that driven by the unions?"

A long pause at the other end, the passing of notes could be heard over the void.

"Yes, but appreciate we won't be communicating that externally."

"I understand that Jack," Steve pushed hard "but we're on full disclosure here."

"Steve, the guys are on it here. Yes, there's some noise in the two depots from the unions. We think we can control it before it gets out of hand."

"Add that one to the memo maybe?" Steve jabbed to more pauses.

"Yep, we can sure do that, some sort of indemnity agreement would probably work for us both I assume?"

Comprehensive nods around the room. Many of the individuals here hadn't even considered covering these angles. Even with the loaded deck, Steve was still able to play both sides better than most could play one.

The briefing continued, final details on the cash injection, designed to get them over the fast approaching Christmas period. Despite it being clear to him that there was no pulling out of this dive for the supplier, he nodded, acting impressed at the details of their recovery.

"So, if there's no further questions?" pausing for effect.

"Fine, get in touch with Siobhan at this end if anything comes up through the day and we can co-ordinate responses. I guess, finally, from me, I would just like to extend the appreciation of the entire board to you John, and Steve, for your continued support. Christ knows where we would be without you, but there's light at the end of the tunnel."

That light is a freight train hurtling towards you, Steve considered, as pleasantries were exchanged and the call was ended.

"Anything TWG, route through Steve today, he's running point." nods of agreement spread round the table. "Let's to it, it's going to be a big couple of weeks."

Steve exited early to avoid further deepening of the conversation around Russell's retirement. There would be time for this once the next part of the plan was in motion. He had grown fonder of the man over the last few months, a rare chink in his armour, and wanted the exit to be managed correctly. It was going to be hard enough on him to lose heavily from his hard earned fortune, so the least Steve could do was make it as soft a landing for him as possible.

"Good morning, boss." the dulcet tones of Rachel swept him back.

"Good morning, Rachel." he smiled the smile, only reserved for her.

"Need me for anything?" leaning into the doorway, she bolted upright as the remaining Directors passed behind Steve, deep in conversation.

"Could do with a cuppa." he smiled again.

"Coming right up, boss." sweeping her hair behind her ear, she brushed past Steve towards the small kitchenette area overlooking the car park.

Although she was much shorter, he caught the scent of her perfume from her slender neck. Her youth both intrigued him, and yet, scared him. Everything about her was different to what he knew, and what he had. She made his mind race, and his heart pound. The electric surges from brief interactions such as this were making him crave more, as dopamine surged his system, his addiction grew.

Slumping back in his chair, he turned his wedding ring yet again. His mind wandered to things at home, they were steady, consistent, but predictable. The comparison alone, between the two worlds, was enough to strike further chemical reactions. There was no real reason to be comparing his life partner and his personal assistant, but yet he was. Imagining the suppleness of the young graduates body, as she entered his office, coffee in hand. He dragged himself back, forcing the thoughts out of his mind, desperate for them to stop projecting through his eyes.

"Coffee, boss."

She smiled. A dancer, or a gymnast, he couldn't figure out, as she gracefully closed the door with one foot, whilst maintaining full balance and composure. Her stunning eyes, bright and wide, full of energy and life. Her long sleeve top fitting in all the right places, as she leant over his desk to place the mug close to him.

It took all Steve could muster to not lose his line of sight down the plunging neckline. He focused hard on the mug. Desperate to convince his own mind she had leaned just far enough, and he shouldn't read anything into it.

"Lovely, cheers!" he tried to dismiss. Eyes from the mug to the screen to his right "Anything urgent for today?"

"Well, only the Christmas party" she paused, pushing both sides of her hair back, running her hands past her neck. "Mags managed to get your room upgraded."

"Mags did?" He startled, unsure of the sudden developments, after years of trying to get something better than an Executive room.

"Well, I might have known the right person to ask." Rachel feigned a wink, now she had his attention again. "My brother works there."

"Oh, that's great, well, thanks, that's great." he stumbled, repressing his drifting mind.

"If there's nothing else?" She asked openly "Then I'll get out of your way."

"Thanks, Rach." watching intently as she turned, and headed to the door.

The ping of his iPad alerted him to the released of the TWG announcement, washing over him like a cold shower. Loading up the ShareWatch page, and splitting the screen between the two businesses in question, he sat back, sipping his piping hot drink. The page refreshed every few seconds, and whilst both the graphs had been declining for the first few minutes of trade, it now began to drop off quicker.

Nothing changed in the minutes that Steve sat there in silence. An occasional levelling off, before the fall continued, like a slinky thrown down a set of stairs, eventually reaching what seemed to be the bottom. Both losing double digit percentages in their price in a matter of hours.

Grabbing the BOSS bag from the floor, he rummaged through for the phone tucked away, whilst keeping an eye on the screen. He foraged around the open pocket, a jolt of electric running through him as he couldn't feel the cold metal. Muscles tightened and his stomach began to twist, chest tightening, he flung his other hand into the bag, staring intently inside as if he was almost sniffing it out.

Huge waves of relief swept through him as he realised he had zipped it in the wrong pocket previously. A tremendous exhale of breath. Fears of others getting hold of the unit subsided as he unlocked it.

Only once before had he received a photo message on this device, the day Mark Jeffries had departed. A picture that had invoked such an emotional response in him, like nothing he had ever felt before. Staring intently at the latest one, the same heightened concoction of anticipation, excitement, pride and fear coursed through him. Steve wished he had kept the whiskey bottle.

Swiftly deleting the message, he carefully made sure the phone was now returned to its correct home. He drained the remainder of the coffee. Checking the bag another time, as he stood to take his daily walk.

He couldn't help but peer his head around the adjacent doorway, just to catch a glimpse. Entering quietly, he just watched. She was miles away, tapping the plastic keys with ease, gliding her elegant fingers across the keyboard while intently engrossed in the screen in front, even this was driving Steve mad. Trying to snap himself out of whatever was going on. Admin had never had this effect on him before.

"Great coffee, Rach." he grinned

"Oh, thanks Steve, I put the granules in myself." A slight jump, she fluttered her eyelashes, tilting her head slightly.

"Can you get Alison to pop in tomorrow?"

"Of course, nice and early? It is Friday after all." she smiled, luring him in for conversation "I'll sort that for you, looks like she's here tomorrow anyway."

Steve turned to walk away.

"Thanks again Rach, it's been great having you here."

Turning briefly back around, Rachel's eyes hurried back to his, after quite blatantly being fixated on his backside. She flustered, shuffling in her seat, before shrugging. A broad, cheeky, grin now came over her, as she slightly raised her right eyebrow; She knew she'd been spotted, she had wanted to be spotted.

Steve's heart pulsated violently in his chest, but it felt more like his throat. He span the wedding band that now felt like it was digging into his skin.

"Can't blame a girl for enjoying the view." she spoke with a confidence matched with a cheeky smile, which both now morphed into brazen flirtation. Such a change from the first time they met.

Rarely was a man of his stature lost for words. He had delivered seminars to thousands of people, even dealt with the advances of other women in the past. All of which he had passed off with relative ease. Right now, Steve Bellingham was a silent, flabbergasted, mess.

"Are you going to leave again or what?" She continued.

"I'll be back later." the grin for her returned, he felt his eyes narrow, observing her, his desires now written clearer than ever across his slightly blushed face.

"You better be." she turned back to her screen, flicking her hair.

Outside the room, he leaned against the wall and exhaled heavily, his mouth directing the air up to his forehead. Temperature raised, flushed cheeks, heart pounding. Desperate to control the surges of conflicting messages shooting around him.

"Get a fucking grip." he whispered to himself.

Shaking himself down, the grip came. His legs began working again, and guided him down towards the trading department. Successfully enough, that he was soon knocking at the new office of Martin Armstrong.

The move was not Steve's first choice, preferring to keep Martin out in his shop facing role, and Alison Maxwell pulling the strings here. However, it hadn't been easy to swing through the board. She had no buying experience, so Steve always knew he needed a plan B, and this was it. Moving Martin across, under the guise of developing and broadening his experience, had opened up the Operations Director role for Maxwell. Something she had richly deserved after the expert career assassination of this office's previous tenant.

Martin had settled in well, and the team seemed to like him, which was a major step. He had promoted the gobby buyer, Lucy, who had been so challenging to Steve previously. A shrewd move which had kept her close enough to stifle any challenge. In that moment, he had earned some rare commendation.

Steve closed the door behind him, and leant against it, as if to keep it closed.

"We need to chat." Steve demanded.

"All ears boss." replied Martin, attempting to hide a sudden onset of anxiety from such an entrance.

8

Steve's Jaguar pulled over the gravel of the lay-by, slowly coming to a halt next to the over flowing concrete bin. Switching off the ignition, he soaked up the noise of cars as they sped past only a couple of meters away, the other side of the row of conifers and empty drink cans. Pulling his bag over swiftly from the back seat, he grabbed the phone hidden at the bottom.

He opened the only message he had on the phone, checking the time at the top of the screen, he tried to connect the call. Surprisingly getting through just before the second ring.

"Steve?" came the female voice on the other end. He detected a hint of emerald isle.

"Niamh, I presume." It began to sank in who he had been connected to.

Niamh Jones, CEO of FreshCo Supermarkets. Only 38, she was now one of the youngest female CEOs in the FTSE 100. They had briefly met at a conference a number of years ago. His clandestine contacts clearly knowing the way to the top of most corporate ladders.

"Ha! This is all a bit cloak and dagger for my liking." she softened some, placing the tone further to the northern part of Ireland.

"Agreed, but it's good to finally be talking." Steve relaxed into his chair, but still checking the rear view mirror.

"Yes, and to you." Niamh replied "Are you free of Russell's clutches yet?"

The Irish woman had little to no time for the Russell's founder. An attempt many years ago to buy the retail group from John, during its fledgling years, had turned their relationship sour. Niamh Jones had seen the potential of the up and coming small shop operator very early on, urging her, then, seniors at FreshCo Supermarkets to snap up the retailer. They themselves had no presence in the small side of food retail, confining their approach to aircraft hanger sized behemoths. She could see then, as a mid-level Head of Business Development, that this would have further cement their place as the number one in the UK.

Up until the recent events, Russell's had gone from strength to strength, proving the strong willed brunette right. As she climbed the ladder at FreshCo, she would demand a return to the table, despite knowing the purchase price was ever increasing. This was now a matter of principal. Sadly, however, she was up against the hard ball King.

John Russell would simply not entertain sitting across the table from her, or her minions. He blocked calls from anyone connected to FreshCo, despite the gigantic payout which he would have received at the height of the company's value.

"I guess you know our history." she continued.

"It's part of the induction here." he chuckled.

"Well look, I'll be honest wit' you now." in her strongest Belfast candour. "We simply do not have the cash flow to come in for another deal, as I'm sure you've already established."

Last year's financial report had been hit by a multi-million pound hole. Years of manipulated accounts, through over valuing of bricks and mortar assets had been found out. Many analysts questioned if their long term auditors had been tipped off to the discrepancy, but the rumour soon drifted. As did both the CFO and CEO, who exited the company very soon after. Allowing Jones to now take her seat at the head of the table.

"But a big wholesale supply would begin to fix that little hole I assume." he calculated swiftly.

"It would indeed." an impressed inflection came through the phone clamped to Steve's right ear. "Internally, it's a bit of a taboo subject"

"Marketing guys running the show? Harping on about brand perception?" Steve smiled, it was rare he found business conversation on his level.

"Like you wouldn't believe." she chuckled "but that's for me to sort. I've locked a few of my people in a room to get things as ready as they can without scaring the horses."

"Like your style." Steve reflected in genuine respect to the younger lady. He relaxed further, switching to his opposite ear, leaning into the leather seat.

"Well, they've got the framework, and what needs to be done. I won't bore you wit' the details." she paused "I obviously need to deal with old stubborn bollocks at your end."

Steve guffawed like he had not in years.

"And that's for me to sort out."

"Yes, well I assumed the manner in which we were connected would mean it was of a slightly more insidious nature." she mused "I won't push, as keen as I am to clear this, particular pathway, shall we say."

Steve hummed acknowledgement, not wanting to give anything away. Call it aversion to risk or whatever, he preferred to keep those cards close to his chest.

"Plausible deniability, I think that's what they call it." she concluded. "So it certainly seems like the right time for us to be talking given Jack's fuck up at TWG. We've got the terms of their supply, don't ask how, not that it was hard I guess, that place is like a leaky bucket right now."

More chuckles from Steve.

"So my project gang have put that into our language." as she meaningfully segwayed into some headline financials.

The deal was as good as the Kingsland deal Jeffries had presented a few months earlier, with no negotiation completed on either part. Steve rubbed his stubbly chin and stared out of the window, watching the cars in the distance arrive at a puddle strewn roundabout. The rain had stopped long before, but standing water forming around the junction, was now being thrown into air, like Stevenage's urban, grey, version of the Bellagio fountains. His one and only visit to Vegas was full of fond, but distant, memories. His proposal to Sarah in the heyday of their relationship in front of those fountains came blearily into his mind, but it was right now, that he felt like he was about hit the jackpot.

"That's a starting point I assume." after a long pause.

"I already prefer you to the old man." she laughed.

"I'll need to secure some capital to really get this through, and your systems will need to be ready." Steve considered, he knew he was pushing it, but a bit of cash to spend around the business would give him even more leverage.

"Systems won't be an issue, 2 weeks and we will be ready." she played a hand she hadn't intended to. This deal, its contrived spontaneity, slowly dissipating.

"How long have you kept them in that room Niamh?"

"Always be prepared, I was taught." She deflected "Capital. Now, I can't do a lot, but the guys tell me I can get to four or five."

"We clearly both like to plan these conversations ahead." Steve attempted to drive home the considerable similarities between the two senior executives.

"Ah, it's a fool that doesn't. Seems like we can get somewhere with that as a starter for ten?" She fished.

"Not a million miles off, that's for sure. Finance boys can tighten the bolts on it, but it's certainly something I can take to the board." Steve considered his pre-judged next steps, cautious and meticulous.

"Good, and official channels next time, for clarity and all that."

"Watch for the white smoke." in deference to her strong Catholic roots.

"Fumata blanca." she declared, smiling. "I'm impressed Bellingham."

With that she ended the call. Steve wiped the phone screen on the leg of his suit trousers, before zipping it away for a new day. She was an impressive operator. From what he knew, what he read, and briefly saw in her occasional slots on 24 hour news. Far from being in awe of the younger woman, he did have a huge dose of admiration for her, and if he were honest, a small pang of jealousy. She had built a career that outstripped his in both its magnitude and speed.

Right now, he needed to summon the board meeting, a congregation that was as far from a papal conclave as were possible, to begin preparations for the inevitable storm they were charging towards. He hit the ignition on the car, and flicked up gravel as he pulled the Jag back onto the main road. Bursting through the puddles, barely checking for traffic at the roundabout, he smiled. Things were going better than planned, he felt invincible.

Meanwhile, Niamh Jones sat back in her kitchen chair, and sipped her cooling glass of green tea. She hated the stuff, but it did its job. Reflecting on the conversation that had just played out, she stood and walked the length of her extended dining room, merging into a beautifully curated conservatory. He was an arrogant man, but not obstinate like the elder in that strange partnership. Bringing up her religion was uncalled for, and somewhat uncouth, but in the moment, it was right to massage such a fragile ego as his. It had served great purpose in refining the character she had built in her mind. Stepping out into the garden, she shouted for her six year old daughter to stop riding the dog, and sipped the last of her acrid drink.

****

The final dregs of coffee poured down his throat, he strode from his vehicle towards the building, full of vigour and resolve. Bounding up to his office, he knocked almost too loudly on Rachel's door, startling her.

"My office, five minutes please." hardly giving her a moment.

Throwing himself into his large leather desk chair, hands behind his head. A long intake of the stuffy office air, that felt as good as any forest breeze, filled his lungs.

"Good meeting?" Entered Rachel into the room, closing the door firmly behind, and acknowledging Steve's euphoric state.

"Always good when you win." he fell forward, elbows onto the desk with a resounding thump. "How was your morning?"

"Me?" She giggled "Must have been a big win."

He was only diarised to be with Saj at Sixtrees, who ironically, was now covering for him rather than highlighting the lies of Mark Jeffries. So the meeting should not really have delivered such an ecstatic return. Steve looked at Rachel, so naive and innocent, she had no idea.

"Superb, I need to get the board together sharpish." he smiled, looking her straight in the eyes. "Needs to be this week."

"I think everyone is free before the party on Friday." her eyes met his, matching his grin.

"Oh shit, yeah the Christmas party, yeah pop something in before that, only needs a couple of hours. I'll make sure John and JT are on board."

"Just don't be late for the party." she winked "Want me for anything else?"

Steve could think of many things in this moment as he stared intently at the beautiful young lady stood before him.

"No, no, don't think so." she turned to leave "What time are you getting there Friday?"

Unsure what deep recess of his mind that came from, the wedding ring spinning returned. A developed tic Steve was now semi-conscious of, this time he stopped himself.

"Oh probably about eight." surprised at her boss's advance "I like to make an entrance."

"And you make an excellent exit too." Steve whispered to himself. "Great." was all she heard as she returned to begin pulling the board together.

Bolton was the linchpin in this now, Steve had determined a while back, much of his work to date had been warming him up for the shit storm about to land on his teams workflows. That poor old dry-wipe board of his would not know what hit it. The IT Director was a sensible guy though, one of the smartest on the board, he had proved that in the Kingsland work. As Steve approached the outhouse, he remained buoyantly confident. Despite the mammoth workload.

"Mr B." Steve called out a few paces from the man's office door, swinging inside and closing it firmly behind him.

"Mr B." Phil replied smirking, pushing his mouse away, whilst checking the time on the screen "What do I owe this pleasure?"

"TWG." Steve threw to the air between them.

"My favourite subject," Phil sighed. "they closing another one?"

"Not quite," he paused "can I talk openly with you?"

Steve checked over his shoulder, purely for effect. Making Bolton feel as if he were part of the Privy Council about to be told the state's darkest secrets, was certainly a way to his heart. The Scotsman lapped it up, leaning further into his desk, intrigue and anticipation etched his wrinkled brow.

"Of course, of course." joining in the eager eyes.

"If they go under, we are not ready." Drawing nods of understanding. "Been on my mind since the call."

"Not gonna lie, I didn't sleep too good that night. What's John's view?"

"Not taken my concerns to him yet, wanted to sound you out first. It hits your team disproportionately hard."

"You're not wrong." a small puff of his chest at the recognition "The guys are at their limit with the switchover of depots."

Steve knew this wasn't entirely accurate. Bolton was skilled in keeping firm control on the amount of work coming in and out of his realm. This usually meant erring on the side of caution.

"Totally." the acknowledgement was never unwelcome this side of the border "Doesn't it feel like we're fixing a crack in the wall when the ceiling is about to fall in?"

"Aye, doesn't it always?" He smirked.

"TWG go under. Then what?" Forcibly bringing him back to the subject

"We've been through this chap, what are you getting at?"

Limited scenarios had been worked up, the most viable being between a hybrid cash and carry and local supply model, or a hugely revised deal with Kingsland which was set up to punish them. They'd get some improvement but would still be a huge step back, and relations were frosty at best. The hybrid model was the only route. Bolton was, on the surface, a fan. Primarily as it actually reduced his teams workload, whilst trebling that of the Finance department. Not that he would take an oath to that effect.

"What if there was another way? Another supply route?"

"From where Steve? TWG are fucked because the big 4 are ripping every last morsel of meat off them." calculating as he spoke. Running through the top 4 supermarkets in his mind "The Germans won't touch us, Thompsons can't get their act together, we fucked Kingsland in the arse, that only leaves…"

The pause grew, as did Steve's smile. Bolton realising where this was going. His eyes narrowed as he considered what the COO was intimating.

"Surely not." now responding to the slow deliberate nod of the senior man "Shit."

"John will hate it."

"No shit Sherlock! But fuck me, I'm more interested in how? What? Who?" Rambled the IT Director.

"They can't talk to John, obviously, but have presented me some headline commercials to consider."

Steve continued through a heavily redacted version of the earlier conversation. Just enough to get his colleague keen. Although Bolton's loyalty had been proved time and time again, this would test it harder than ever before. It would mean going up against the main man, a point he saved until the end of his monologue.

"Not a chance."

Steve paused, waiting for some glint of Glaswegian humour.

"Not a chance, Steve." Bolton repeated, dashing that hope "in that timescale as well? Christ man!"

"They've got a strong team, and can do most of the heavy lifting." regretting the words as soon as they left his mouth.

The IT man was less than impressed at Steve's insinuation the technical aspects would be handled by the FreshCo team. Letting him know in a short, succinct, burst of expletives. The suggestion it would be managed in house seemed to add fuel to the burning flame. Bolton reddened, rubbing his temples, in frustration.

"12 weeks Steve, best case! 12 weeks! Get me some temps yesterday and I might be able to cut a week or two, but shit! We're already a couple of weeks into some of the hybrid systems."

"You're going to need to make it work." he snapped "At some point this isn't going to be negotiable."

"Steve, you don't get it, you don't understand the programming involved, getting our data into someone else's system safely and accurately."

"I suggest you start finding a way."

Bolton finally found some restraint. More through exacerbation than a measured control of his Scottish temper.

"Steve, I think we're done, otherwise I'm going to say something I regret."

Without conclusion, Steve stepped back into the outside area between the two buildings. Whilst Bolton was not going to be a walkover, he hadn't planned for such an obstinate rebuttal, he pounded the pavement towards the sleek car parked a few meters away. Unlocking it, he opened the passenger door and reached inside without really looking. He popped open the glove box and pulled out the two items he needed, shoved them into his suit pockets, and looked around. Slamming the compartment closed, then dealing the same to the car door.

Remotely he secured it all up and walked around the side of the IT block. He slowed his pace, which had been furiously driven by frustration at his failure to read Bolton, but primarily by the Scot's shortsighted stupidity, lack of respect, and blatant insubordination. He had kowtowed to the man one to many times for this.

From where he stood, he had full sight through the man's office window, although a number of meters away, he could see his balding silhouette against the blue white light of his monitor. Steve reached into his pockets, the cold against his hand startled him briefly, it had been a while since he had his fingers running over the brushed metal. Pulling it out, he flicked the catch, checking that it still worked. It had been a long time coming.

Lighting the cigarette, he felt a twinge in his chest. A response to the months without nicotine coursing through his body. He had smoked heavily through his late teens and into his twenties. Vowing to stop after seeing the ravaging effects of the addiction on his paternal grandfather but the thrill never really subsided.

He stared at the stunning pewter, engraved lighter, as he inhaled deep and strong on the remainder of the stub in hand. Blowing the toxic smoke up into the air above, watching it drift against the makeshift shelter, and off into the trees above.

Returning his gaze back to Bolton's outline, thoughts crossed his mind on how to tackle the situation. A misguided loyalty to Russell, which would now prove to be his weakness. He had angered Steve beyond reproach, for all the years of patronage towards the man. This loyalty should have been towards him, and now he would pay the cost.

Russell now needed to be in the right mindset for Friday's board meeting, which meant turning up the heat on him directly. Steve dubbed out the last of the burning embers onto the tree next to him, and disposed of the butt in the clumps of untended weeds behind, and set off to find the man who had given him true loyalty.

9

"The pack was superb Martin, really eye opening! Pass on my thanks to Lucy. She's done a great job." Russell expressed.

She had. Clearly one of the brightest, if more challenging, minds on the department, Martin had insisted she be behind the speedy collation of a TWG review pack. Presenting this to Russell a couple of hours prior to the meeting they now sat in, gave the information a chance to sink in.

"We clearly have a bigger issue than we first thought," he continued, staring at Steve "or were made to believe."

Clearly, Steve needed to take some heat in this situation. For all intents and purposes, he had missed some information regarding the cost base at TWG, combined with some increased pressure from the unions which had flared up in the last 24 hours. In Russell's eyes, Steve should have been first with this info. He sat and said nothing.

"Thanks John, I agree, it gives us a good insight." Martin responded. "If you all flick to the last page, Lucy and I have collated a bit of a litmus test on the previous options we worked up in this room."

The other Directors all took their cue and turned through their decks.

"Martin showed me this earlier, and I really wasn't keen."

Both men chuckled.

"Clearly the hybrid model gives us some real headaches," Armstrong paused "but overall the most suitable here and now is a direct switch. Appreciating that people aren't queuing at the door to supply us right now."

With a climbing, but still low share price, vultures were circling. Takeover proposals, or winding up orders, looked more likely to arrive through the reception postbox at this point.

"Finding the right partner may not be impossible, Lucy has had some interesting opening dialogue with the Germans, and a couple of the smaller fully integrated guys. All of which have wholesale systems ready to go. Thompsons would like a meeting."

Nods of acceptance around the room, but still nobody spoke. Tension course through the shoulders of Phil Bolton, as clearly highlighted, at the top of the risk list across all options, was reference to his department.

"Phil, chat us through the IT infrastructure points," Russell opened "clearly understand you've got pressures but some of these timings seem to leave us exposed."

Bolton launched into a tense, defensive, but relatively controlled, monologue about the timing issues. With less expletives than had been aimed at Steve a couple of days previously, he tried to convince the room he was under resourced to complete any of the switchovers. The only suitable option was to push on with the hybrid model. The finance representatives twisted in their seats, ready to strike, but Steve took up pole position, staring down Bolton.

"The alternative supply routes show that a number of these businesses have their own existing plug in systems as Martin mentioned." Pausing for the room to prepare for the fireworks. "what stops us plugging in to that?"

Bolton was about to speak, when Russell interjected.

"I've heard these plug ins can take just a couple of weeks."

It took a concerted effort from both Martin and Steve to restrain from smiling. Their, somewhat, subtle references to Russell about how other businesses had linked up in this way, and the capabilities of many of these had resonated deep in his memory, and now he had pulled out the Queen of hearts.

Bolton stumbled to answer, frustration, like a cornered rat, he snapped at Steve, verbally swiped at Martin, refraining from taking on Russell.

"Phil, this isn't Steve and Martin's battle," he drew the line "this is for all of us. The future of our company."

"What you are asking is not possible, the data integrity, the reliability, everything" he began throwing his hands around, blood rushing through his face "we will hand everything over to FreshCo."

The mention of their name alone caused a seething consternation within the company elder. His jolly freckled face, now running flecks of purple, his veins visible.

"We are not going with fucking FreshCo, Phil, stop with the conspiracy theories." Clearly Bolton had been trying to work an angle with the raging, bullish, CEO "The guys here have done what your team should have been doing for fucking weeks. Finding bloody solutions."

Battle lines were drawn, and Russell had put himself on Steve's side. Phil might have planned on this allegiance to see him through, but he hadn't considered that his allies were as open to change. As the new facts had been presented, John Russell had seen sense. Now he was scrambling to maintain control, to stop the careering juggernaut from going over the edge, and wiping out his department with it.

"Or whoever then, John." realising Steve had already diffused this bomb "The implications are huge, our data everywhere, redundancies widespread across IT, supply, operations, the list is endless."

Desperation swept the IT man's body language. Now imploring others to believe him, let alone join his side of the fight. There were no takers, heads dropped to avoid eye contact. He had battled this argument too long, taken on the wrong parties, and now he was wounded.

"I'm not taking it Phil. I'm rarely this fucking direct, but circumstances have forced my hand here. Get your fucking team in order, and get me a plan to prepare our systems."

Russell clearly didn't know the detail on how to complete such a task, but he had been fed enough from those around the table, and also a convenient call from an acquaintance earlier in the day. His network of industry alumni was strong, so a chance call from the former Supply Chain Director at Kingsland, initially asking for some career advice, had given him a better foundation of understanding on which to form his staunch position. Silence hit the room. Eerie at first, how it must be after an explosion. Russell's words still ringing in everyone's ears.

"This is bigger than all of us, bigger than one department or another." He looked to address the full table, elevating himself back to the alpha. "We will only survive, this business will only fucking survive, if we make the right decisions in this room."

His stubby index finger pounded into the table, with surprising force, as if hammering the statement deep into the wood for posterity.

Glancing at the simmering Scotsman, Russell could see the mans disconnect from the call for action, preferring to wallow in his own petulance. There were times that leaders of companies were required to be somewhat selfless, for the greater good, and there were times when only the fittest survived.

Shockwaves reverberated for the remaining few moments of the meeting. Bolton playing no part, other than scribbling notes whilst slumped back in his chair, as he chewed the inside of his bottom lip furiously.

"Can I see you John?" He blurted as those around him stood, packing away their items.

"Later, Phil." Russell dismissed, as he headed to the door. Steve firmly by his side.

Both men strode meaningfully up the stairs as to make ground between them and the man standing helpless at the bottom.

"I don't appreciate being in that position, Steve." Russell flared as he entered his office, Steve closing the door behind them with a deep breath.

"John, please."

"No, I'm not done." He pointed "You gave me no option in there, you and Martin knew that. What else could I do? I had to back you, and now the line is drawn. I truly hope you know what you've got yourself, and this company, into!"

"He's only out to cover his own arse John."

"I don't deny it, but he's earned that right. There was better ways of playing that Steve, I mean talk to the man for fuck sake!"

Russell sat, and looked out of the side window to Steve's left, fingers perched in a tent like shape, tipped against his lips.

"The facts are the facts John, he's stalling, delaying, whatever, to try and cover his own arse. It's putting the company at risk. You know he won't listen to reason, especially from me."

"Yes he is." Russell now fighting Steve's argument for him "Put yourself in my shoes. What would you do?"

"Exactly the same. Including this." he smiled, pointing at the pair with an open palm.

Russell smiled wryly, a huffed laugh signalled that the tension between the two men would not last long. He had just needed to get that off his chest, irritation at having to change stance, and give a dressing down to, now, one of his longer serving board members. His fingers rubbed his tired eyes.

"What's next, oh Oracle?"

Steve chuckled, he'd only called him this a couple of times before.

"A couple of beers, and some average hotel food, followed by the obligatory drunken pitch for promotion. Who have you go on the sweepstake for that?"

What seemed like every Christmas party, one member of the junior office team would get steaming drunk, and approach multiple members of the board, slurring a semi prepared speech about how they should be promoted. A mock sweepstake had been discussed between them as to this years culprit.

Both men chuckled, Steve eventually allowed to sit as they mused the evenings activities. Eventually, Steve was able to depart to deal with more pressing matters. Skimming past Rachel's side office he noted she had departed a little earlier than normal. To be expected, he considered, the office became a very male dominated world just before 5pm on the day of any dressy event.

He himself managed to depart only an hour and half later. Deciding to let the dust settle on the afternoon's meeting, and get some rest before the evening's festivities. With dinner planned for 8pm, he would afford himself a rare rest in the expansive hotel bed which greeted him. Throwing his Tom Ford suit carrier over the back of the black faux leather chair, he let himself fall face first into the thick cotton sheets, rolling to his side briefly to fire off a text to Sarah, and set an alarm, before returning and closing his eyes.

The incessant techno music woke him blearily, hardly an hour later. In that moment, he regretted taking the short break, but he knew later, as the drink was flowing, he would value it. Rolling onto his feet, he stripped off and stepped into the shower, letting the hot water pass over the back of his neck, and sporadically run down his face.

Finished, he wrapped his lower half in the warm hotel towel, and stood in front of the large mirror. He stared at his physique, and thought of Rachel. Considering how she had made eyes at him previously, and wondered why. He was not an overly handsome man, well built, with broad shoulders that belied a slight hop-induced podge around the waistband. His face had a constant tired look to it, shadows took up residence under his eyes and down the top of his nose.

Trimming his stubble to his preferred length, he preened himself until the view was a little more acceptable, before donning his designer tuxedo. A few flashes of the fingers later and his bow tie looked perfect. Way better than the shop bought clip-on ones, he thought, and these ones looked great when undone. Like a corporate, aged, James Bond, he stood bolt upright in the mirror, and pulled his trigger fingers.

His room was in one of the smaller outbuilding blocks at the manor style hotel. A brightly lit archway of pruned ivy led him to the main building. Following the reverberating bass, and hubbub of office gossip, he entered the room for the night's festivities. The wave of party music and colourful flashing lights hit him, they mixed with a heady aroma of cheap lager to create an attack on almost all the senses. Glancing around the room, he smiled politely at those he grazed eye contact with, whilst lifting a small Champagne flute, filled with Prosecco, from the silver tray on his right.

Walking across the, already sticky, wooden floor, he greeted more and more people until he reached his destination. The small huddle of Directors hiding near the corner of the bar area. Most of them had arrived by now, however Bolton was notable in his absence, as he chose to stand a few yards away animatedly conversing with his leadership team.

Conversation, and making way for waiters had turned Steve to be facing back the way he came. Disco lights swirled, and spots of brilliant light spun around the walls, brushing past his eyes causing him to wince. Occasionally it matched the rhythm or beat of music, but that was only by chance, it seemed.

Then all of a sudden it all stopped. A vision of blonde appeared in the doorway, bright yellow lights framed her shapely figure, which was hugged by a tight blue jersey dress. He couldn't help but stare, something she noticed, but intentionally avoided. She made small talk conversation with the group that accompanied her, glancing occasionally to check that his eyes were still firmly on her.

"Drink, boss?" came Martin's voice over the incessant beat. Making Steve realise it was he that had stopped, not the party.

"Pint of..." he scanned the makeshift bar of cheap branded lagers "anything, cheers!"

Finishing his allocation of cheap fizz, he placed the glass on the table behind him, before returning his focus to the doorway. Scanning the area, he realised she had gone. Mingling somewhere in the hoard of department store glamour.

The thudding of hand on microphone bought most to attention, reducing the noise to a more manageable level. A few more taps of Russell's hand on the DJs equipment got the desired attention level, matched with a few discreet nudges on those who had drunk a little more already.

Everyone was invited to take their seats, Steve scanned the room of tables for Rachel. She was nowhere to be seen, until he reached his table at the very front of the converted conference room. There she was, radiant against the rainbow of disco lighting. Slowly seating herself on Steve's table, he grinned.

"I'm guessing someone thought we should get to know each other a bit more." he smoothly approached, taking the seat next to her.

Her face flushed red as she smiled. Leaning in so her response could be heard by him, and him alone.

"Well you won't hear me complaining." she uttered, before removing her hand from his thigh.

Conversation flowed between the pair over the atypical, bland, batch cooked chicken meal presented to them by less than enthusiastic hotel staff. Steve keeping her smiling and laughing the whole way through to dessert.

"I'll come find you later for a dance." Rachel whispered as the final dishes were cleared away, and disappeared into the crowded dance floor.

As Steve stood, a smell of heavy whiskey breezed in over his shoulder, he turned to see Phil Bolton hovering over him.

"I'm sure your wife would love to know about your PA there, Steve." he slurred, the strong smell only intensifying on his hot breath.

"Phil, you're pissed." Steve sidestepped to move his way round the Glaswegian.

"Fucking nonce." Bolton sniggered.

He stood, slurping the remains from between the ice in his glass. Some of which formed beads that ran down the left side of his lips onto his chin. Wiping it away with the loosened sleeve of his sweat ridden white shirt.

"You know what your problem is?" He continued, raising his voice, and catching the attention of a small group to their side.

"Phil. Stop." Steve turned to face him, closing in, so his mouth was next to his ear "You're fucking pissed, and making a fool of yourself."

The heavy bump of his shoulder hardly threw him off his stride, but caused its dealer to stagger noticeably. Steve continued to walk towards the bar at the back of the room.

"Bellingham." came the muffled slur behind him, increasing in volume "Steve."

Steve paused, allowing Bolton to reach him, smiling to diffuse the tension created by more groups turning to watch. The drunken Scot now invading his personal space, two inches more than would be appropriate. The aroma of cheap scotch was pungent.

Steve wanted nothing more than to bounce the jumped up Scot off the partition walls surrounding them. He had expected more of him after many years.

Disgusted at the times he had kowtowed to him in meetings, supported his elaborate requests, even defending him multiple times to Russell.

"Phil, you're embarrassing yourself." Steve leaned in once more. Controlling his temper's desire for a fight.

"You think you got all this in your hand don't you Steve? Got John playing puppet now, Steve? Tidy little PA to have some fun with, Steve?" Goaded the bedraggled drunken IT man.

"You're playing a game, Steve and I can see it, even if nobody else can, you played me."

"Phil, I'm not playing you." Steve stared down the barrel "Last piece of advice from me. Go to bed, sleep this off."

"Oh and Jeffries, let's talk about Jeffries shall we?" Bolton's voiced raised above the murmurs around them.

"Come on Phil, let's get some air." Martin Armstrong appeared at the side of the 2 men.

Whisking him off out the door, Steve lingered for a few minutes, ensuring that all conversation returned to relative normal, before he followed after the men. The smoking shelter was not far from the main room, and as he approached down the glass lined corridor, he could see the men animatedly talking. Measuring his steps, and slowing his pace he made time before his approach, through the, propped open, fire exit doors.

"I'll leave you two to it." Martin shuffled away.

"Let's walk." Steve demanded, nodding a thanks at Martin for his bail out.

The sounds from the room subsided as they walked from the shelter. Occasional bass filled beats, or sounds of drunken cheering could be heard. The air was cold, so much so, that both men puffed blooms of vapour as they walked, despite the lack of cigarettes.

"I ain't pissing around Steve." started Phil, still slurring slightly, but more in control of his balance than before. "I know about Jeffries."

Steve chose not to react, kept his eyes forward, if briefly fixated on the gravel passing beneath his feet.

"Don't worry, I didn't tell your little mini-me." flinging his head back in the direction they came from, causing him to wobbly slightly.

"What you rambling about Phil?" Steve kept focused and calm, despite the bubbling emotions beneath his cold exterior.

"Don't get me wrong, I never really liked him that much either. A pain in my arse as well you know." Continuing as if Steve hadn't interjected. "But, through it all, it was you I didn't trust. When all that shit about Mark came out, it was you that I couldn't work out."

Steve fought to control floods of chemicals flying through his system, mixed with the small amount of alcohol he had consumed, washing around his stomach as it mixed with the stodgy dinner. He could feel his body tensing. Desperate to not signal Bolton's thought trail was leading somewhere significant.

"Fucking hell Phil, what conspiracy theory you throwing my way?"

"I've just never trusted you. Too polished. You're fake." Bolton delivered calmly "These little pawns you have, you move them around as you want, I was never going to be one of them Steve."

"Stop fucking bumbling, and spit it out like a man." Steve broke.

"You did it." Bolton landed.

Stopping dead in his tracks, slightly in front, he turned to stare Steve in the eyes. His shoulders leading the slightest of sways. As the short rose bush next to them rustled in the night breeze. A darkened window casting a reflecting light of the moon on the pair.

"You did it. You set him up." Pointing his hairy finger at parts of Steve's face as he moved.

"Phil, you sound like some drunk, conspiracy nut job right now." chortled Steve.

"You sent that email, well, one of your cronies did it for you." waving his hand around as if the whole world were included. "Delayed send Steve."

"Fucking ridiculous!"

"Delayed send. The actual email was sent at five that morning. I thought something was fishy, so I went fishing." Bolton laughed

Panic ran through Steve, causing a shiver to begin in his leg, and travel up through his stomach to his chest. He pulled his suit jacket together to pass it off as a chill. Rolling his eyes for added effect.

"Jeffries didn't swipe in until six forty. There were only a few people in the building at that time though Steve. I thought it was funny how you were two hundred miles north, but Alison wasn't was she Steve?"

Steve froze to the spot.

"So here's the thing, I cleaned up your little attack dogs mess. Not that John would know what the fuck I'm on about." Bolton joined the eye rolling. "Jack Frost got your tongue Steve?"

Confusion waved through Steve. Unable to decipher his next move quick enough. He pictured bouncing the man off the large rock a few meters in front, calculating if he could get away with it, pass it off as a drunken fall.

"So, there's no evidence. If that's what you're trying to work out there," flinging his hand "other than what I'm keeping, you got close though, I wanted to take it to Jeffries. Show him that little thing called a data access request."

"I'll humour you." Steve paused. "Why didn't you?"

"Because you can protect me." Bolton turned out facing the sky, blowing plumes of dewy breath towards the moon.

"Blackmail." chuckled Steve sadistically, being played was like black humour to him.

"Dirty word that Bellingham. Insurance. I prefer that. When you came storming in the other day, it made my mind up for me. You're better use alive than you are dead."

"Fucking coward."

"Now, now." Confidence rising through the scotch "I'm not asking much, considering. Fuck, I'll even get in line with the FreshCo deal. Just keep me at that fucking table."

"Fuck!" Steve announced, wiping his dry face with his hands "You manipulative little twat."

"Pot, kettle, Steve."

The two men stood in the night, the increased tempo of music highlighted the progression of the evening. More alcohol would be flowing, and much more spilled. Wandering hands of office administrators on the dance floor. The younger staff ordering taxis to the nearest club. Rachel would be there, he was sure. He was stuck here, staring over fields of black, with a scotch field Glaswegian.

"So when we moving on Russell?" Asked Bolton, as if joining the unseen plans in Steve's head.

Steve ignored the comment, staring deeply at the inky horizon, still weighing his options. His fear and anxiety had somewhat passed, but anger remained.

"Fuck it. Play any kind of shit on me again, or threaten me again, and I'll fucking end you." Steve turned, square chested against the slightly smaller, still swaying, Bolton.

"Deal." he announced, faking a spit onto his hand and reached out towards Steve.

Steve brushed past the hand, and stormed off, crunching through the gravel path. He could hear further expletives from the IT Director behind him, ended with a loud chuckle. Powering past the smoker's shelter, wishing he could join, he powered through the exit door, still propped open by a half drunk bottle of red.

He paused for a second outside the main hall, a scene of drunkenness and mild debauchery. Scanning the room swiftly, he missed Rachel catching sight of him and smiling.

Turning, he continued to pound the carpet to the other side of the main building. Pushing open the door to the ivy lined tunnel, it rattled on its hinges at the impact, before softly closing back on itself. By that time, he was fumbling in his pocket for the paper-wrapped plastic keycards. Hammering them on the reader, the wait for the green light felt like an age. Eventually the components inside whirred and he slammed down the handle.

Throwing his jacket over the desk chair in front, he began tugging senselessly at his bow tie. Eventually it came undone and he could unbutton the top of his shirt. Letting out a primal roar of frustration at the insulate man he now had hanging over him, he powered his fist into the laminate desk in front of him. The shockwave reverberated through the desk, as well as its neighbours, causing the glass bottles of water to clink and fall, and the television to wobbly unsteadily on its stand.

It was then that a knock came at the door. Rubbing his reddening fist, he made his way over, opening it without sight.

"Where's my dance?"

She stood there, clearly a good way through the bottle of white they had opened at the table. Rosy cheeked, a glint in her lusciously pale blue eyes. In her hand, a bottle of Champagne and two glasses. The real deal.

Steve held the door without a word, letting her make her way in. Walking like a new born deer in her high heeled shoes. She'd removed them for dancing, but felt a need to wear them here. She sat on the edge of the large bed, taking in her surroundings, before crossing her long bare legs and looking straight at Steve.

Hands in his pocket, Steve was furiously turning the wedding ring on his finger. Imagination racing. He eased it off his finger, leaving it to drop to the bottom of the silk lining as he reached out for one of the glasses.

10

Dawn in the Yorkshire Dales was as beautiful a sight as anything in the world, Niamh considered to herself as she rested her bike against the old stone wall. The pub car park had a breathtaking view. That along, was worth the ride up. A hidden gem on the hilly outskirts of Bakewell. She stood staring over the rising hills and sinking vales, the only real way of clearing her head after a stressful week.

The back channel proposal to Bellingham had gone well. She was confident he had the balls to take on Russell and clear that little ginger road block. Her own board were the real fight, how she loathed the middle-aged male privilege that sat around the glass table in front of her every week. A sign of everything that was wrong with the business.

They were hesitating. Here was the new, young, progressive, and deeply intelligent CEO. All the makings of a tour de force for the industry, who could change the landscape appearing before them, in their favour. FreshCo had been flatlining, the scandal had caused them irreparable damage financially, but also impacted how they were perceived to the every day person.

Therefore, she felt the board should be grabbing her with both hands, and raising her like Simba above the desert. Every opportune moment seized to demonstrate their family values, a marketeers paradise. The difficulty was, she was female. The stuffy old men despised it, in their double breasted suits, hereditary Directors, defined by a long gone time, could not stand to be led by a powerful mother of two.

Freewheeling through the country lanes back to her grossly oversized, extended, cottage gave her the moment of freedom she craved. From the business, from constant emails, and from balancing the needs of a husband, two children, and three dogs. Nobody could control her, except for a few Sunday morning drivers managing to take some sections slower than her. Checking her cyclists watch for the time, she knew she was making great progress.

Breathing in the fast, fresh air. She considered the gathering storm, her place in the centre of it. Things were going to move at such pace in the coming few days, just as she was on the steeper of the downhill stretches.

Down the narrow carriageway, she could make out the lay-by, and the outline of a black vehicle. Closing in at pace, she began to lightly tap her brakes. As she did, the four overlapping circles began to become clear in the morning light. The black Audi was correct, and the last three letters matched what she had been sent the evening before.

Slowing further, she pulled into the elongated lay by. The lights were off in the car, but she could now make out the outline of someone clad in a black coat in the drivers seat, the window fully down even in the freshness of a Yorkshire morning. Approaching the side of the car, her wheels clicked at the slowing of pace, until she came to a stop alongside the open window.

Pulling her small rucksack round to the front, she unzipped the compartment and pulled out the sealed, white padded envelope. No markings, but silently, both parties knew their role. Closing her bag again, she flung it around her shoulder, feeding her arm awkwardly through the other side. She waited as the driver placed the package on the passenger seat and started his engine. Nodding at the him as she set off to leave, but the gesture was not returned.

Barely had she left the lay-by, when the powerful Audi sped past her, the tinted windows rolled up. Up ahead it took the bend recklessly in the middle of the road, which caused a tutted head shake from the cyclist.

Moments later and she was pulling up at the gates to her property. Buzzing her key ring fob against the reader, the motors began to slowly retract the ornate ironwork. She eased through, wheeling the bike along with her hands, walking up the slope towards the double garage. A simple click on the same fob now began opening the cantilever door.

Inside, she hung her bike on the custom stands that also housed the slightly dustier ones of her husband

and children. Packing it away, she hung her bag on the back of the door that connected to the main part of the cottage.

Not that this could be considered much of a cottage any more. The heart of it was still there, but the double garage, extended kitchen, and summer house had all been added in recent years. Preferring to put her money into bricks and mortar than possessions and trinkets.

Her other properties were purchased with the same intentions. Something that could be handed down to the girls over time, somewhat protected against many of the winds of change.

"Mummy!" squealed the excited auburn haired child now clinging to her lycra clad leg.

"Tea's on the side." came the husky male voice from over the breakfast bar.

She stepped forward, leaning over the bowl of fruit and kissed her handsome muscular husband on the lips. Screams of disgust from the two children as they sped across the stone flooring into another room, the dogs chasing close behind.

No more needed to be said to the former professional rugby player who now stood alongside her, arm around her sweaty shoulders. He kissed her on the forehead, and she smiled. Lifting her hot glass of tea, she headed towards the expanse of glass that made the rear of their home, and looked over their small view of perfection.

****

Steve woke grumpily. The weekend had been a write off, a mix of hangover and guilt pained him throughout. Luckily, Sarah had been away for the duration, at her parents house. Dealing with the illness of her mother, and supporting her somewhat frail father. Whether or not, this was the blessing it initially seemed, Steve had wrestled with for 48 hours now. The silent emptiness had left him alone, purely with his thoughts. These flew rapidly between the fracas with Bolton, the liaison with Rachel, and its resultant guilt.

It was that subconscious self-condemnation that had woken him an hour before his normal Monday alarm. Sitting up in bed, finally with a clearer head, he churned over the recent events. However, even that, and the subsequent hot shower did little to resolve his confusion. Slipping into his last ironed white shirt, he made his way downstairs, ignoring the photos of marital bliss as he did. Never one for breakfast, he grabbed a browning banana from the bowl, and made for the door, bag in hand.

Pulling into the company car park, earlier than most mornings, something felt out of place. As he drove around the side of the main building, that feeling manifested itself. Seeing Russell's car here so early turned Steve's stomach. Rarely was he in at this time, let alone the CEO.

Taking the long way round to his office, he could see that Russell's door was slightly ajar. Walking closely, there was no sound behind, no tapping of keyboards, no conversation, just silence. He knocked hard enough so that it opened a little wider. Enough to see the older man jolt in his seat.

"Fucking hell Steve, nearly gave me a heart attack!" Catching his breath, he chuckled.

"Couldn't sleep?"

"Not really, old chap." turning back to the window, comfortable in Steve's presence. "It's niggling me about TWG."

"Talk it out." he perched on the table.

The two shared their concerns about the fragility of their supply partner. Russell appeared still riled by the Friday meeting, he had been almost invisible at the evening event. For whatever fear and trepidation he was dealing with, it was being presented to the outside world as cold combative assault. His fighting spirit had stepped up a couple of notches, wanting to lead the charge from the front.

"I want to get everyone together this morning, address it head on." he considered "They need to hear it from me, from my mouth."

Steve despised the idea. Russell was clearly taking root, getting a strong foundation ready for the storm. Roots that would be harder to dig up in a couple of days.

"There's a lot of uncertainty down there John, no denying that! The rumour mill is working overtime, you could just hear it on Friday, but we need more answers for them. Half answering one question will only make more."

"I guess you're right." he sighed "But, I need to be leading this business, being here, being visible."

Eventually, they agreed to draft and distribute a holding statement for the moment, and prepare a full briefing if it would need deploying. Should TWG wobble and fall this week, then at least the few hundred people under this roof would know they had no solution. Steve rolled his eyes as he exited, bag slung over his shoulder.

There was still silence through the hallways of the building, lights still dimmed, doors still closed. To his relief, that also included Rachel's.

For now, Steve had to focus on dealing with a duplicitous IT Director. He reached into his bag for his covert Apple device.

Update?

Read the only text on the display. The pressure around the small group of individuals involved with him, behind this private number, would be growing.

Stubborn. Need 48 hours.

He replied, almost pre-empting the reply that came after seconds.

24. The hull is breached.

As much was expected, reference to the issues at TWG meant the countdown was on. Steve had a day to force Russell to take the FreshCo deal that would quickly become necessity, but sensed he would likely need the old man to fall on his own sword.

Hearing a rustle from the room next door, the clunking sound of a large handbag on a cheap chipboard desk alerted him to the fact Rachel had arrived for the morning. He hadn't seen her since Saturday morning, waking up next to her, both fuzzy headed from the second bottle of Champagne they ordered on room service.

She had still been asleep, her flowing golden hair spread out over the pillows. He had left her to sleep, and crept into the shower. Trying to wash off the guilt of his actions, he stood, eyes closed and hands pressed against the wall in front. Letting the hot water flow over his head and down his back for what seemed like an age.

Initially, their exchange had been awkward, a mixture of residual alcohol and pounding heads driving the confusion of how to deal with such situations. Something that was portrayed multiple times on television and cinema screens, but in reality, there was little to teach either of them how to react. Steve hoped that the awkwardness in that moment would serve them better this morning.

"Morning, Rachel." Steve's voice offered a hint of flirtation under its professional tone.

"Good morning, Steve." something that was reciprocated in part by the attractive blonde. "Coffee?"

She smiled at his nod, and brushed closely past him as she made her way out of her office door. He couldn't help himself but smell her hair as it drifted past him, clouded flashbacks of the night they shared filled his vision. His wedding ring felt like it was burning into his finger.

Spinning it in his pocket as he walked, mug in hand, down the stairs to the boardroom. Bolton entered from the corridor to his left, catching his eye and flashing him a sadistic grin. Clearly he had been waiting for this moment, believing he had the COO wrapped around his middle finger, which he was subconsciously raising in Steve's face.

A forced greeting to the man to keep appearances, more than anything else, was lapped up with his continued smarminess. He slithered into the room ahead of Steve and grinned a warm greeting to John

Russell, already sat working through documents for the meeting. This took the founder by surprise after Friday's events. Moments passed as everyone sat and cleared up any small talk. Stories were shared to see who would be deemed winner of the office party drunken sweepstakes this year.

"Let's crack on." Russell eyeballed the others intently, solemnly bringing everyone to order.

"We don't have much time to piss around with memories of Friday, although clearly some of you enjoyed yourselves more than others." he continued, before casting his eyes to his pad, leaving the Directors to look around at each other for the unnamed culprit.

"Our favourite subject is the main point this morning. TWG. Steve, fill us in where we are."

Leaving the man sat to his right to outline any updated positions from the weekend. A proposed picket on Saturday at Bristol depot had hit their transit teams, deliveries were missed, and stock wasted. Steve took things carefully, aware of his clandestine text messages giving more time-lined details, although he did enjoy the buzz as he summed up.

"Basically, there's a hole in the ship, and they are taking on water."

"Thanks, as Steve says, they've suffered hard over the weekend. I've tried calling Jack, and no answer." Russell clearly concerned "He's never not answered my calls."

"Let's not forget the taxman is knocking at the door too." came the bored voice of the company CFO. "It's not the unions that will sink the boat Steve."

The dour, pale, man had coughed up this comment at just about every meeting about TWG, as if anyone around the table was unaware. Their VAT deferral was expiring, and despite furious negotiations, it was unlikely they would be granted much more time. The unions had seen the opportunity to grab headlines, and highlight the human side of their problems.

"So at best we have a week, two?"

"A week would be pushing it." came the back up from finance.

"Every time we sit here that gets fucking shorter." Russell complained. "Phil, any changes your side?"

Smiling, the IT Director looked up from the desk, the smile grew as he eyeballed Steve, before turning to Russell.

"A couple of the guys were in over the weekend working on something." Bolton revelled in the light from Russell's face, "We can pull off a switch in a couple of weeks if needed."

The Scot let his gaze linger on Steve as positive reactions echoed through the room. A look of expectation crossing his face., a raised eyebrow. He had teed him up, expecting the COO to now land the FreshCo proposal, and the argument to begin.

"Great stuff, Phil." was all he got.

"Martin, where are you and Lucy at?" Russell pushed.

Little update came through, visibly disappointing Russell, and causing any sense of positivity in the room to leave as quick as it had appeared. Steve, on the other hand, was delighted with the update, as it had bought him the time he needed. It wouldn't look great on Martin for now, but that wouldn't matter soon.

"Disappointed Martin, who did you speak to over the weekend? Anyone? Or just nursing your head? Fucking hell!" Russell was on his own emotional rollercoaster.

A phone buzzed on the table.

"It's Jack." Russell stood, answering the call "I'll be in my office. Steve."

A directive finger that Steve needed to follow, and the meeting was prematurely over.

Despite the clambering of Phil Bolton to get in his ear, he managed to dismiss his advances and catch up with Russell just as he got into his chair. Clicking the door shut quietly once he was inside.

"OK Jack, I understand, look, Steve's here now. I'll fill him in and we can come back to you." Russell ended the call warmly, before turning to Steve. "They are bringing in the administrators."

An inability to negotiate credit terms with key manufacturers, and the tax bill shaped sword of Damocles hanging over them, proving just too big a mountain for them to climb.

A strange mix of fear and admiration waved through Steve as he soaked in the news he had been waiting for. The surreptitious network behind his mysterious text messages had never been fully revealed to him. They were just a number on a screen that never changed. It had connected him to problem solvers in an instant, and whilst the collapse of TWG was necessary in the wider plan, the scale and speed of their actions was formidable.

"We're fucked, Steve." Russell sighed.

"Anything left from Friday?" Steve chuckled sadistically. John continued to stare at the map on his wall.

"We've got a long day ahead Steve." half addressing the comment. "Martin needs to get his finger out of his fucking arse and sort something. The Germans? The northern numpties? What the hell was he doing all weekend?"

Sitting in silence, hoping to take this as rhetorical musings from the boss, Steve refrained from revealing that Martin's lack of activity was at his behest.

Russell began pacing the length of the room, frequently returning to the floor to ceiling map, framed up on the wall. Eventually he stopped there, and studied it harder. It was clear to Steve that he was delving into his memory for any snippets of meetings or contacts he had that may be able to solve their problem. Like the inner workings of Steves watch, the cogs turned at varying speeds. Some useful, and some not so. Remaining in silence, he hoped that the conversation would return to his desire to step away into the sunset.

"Armstrong needs to bring us a solution by the end of the day." not lifting his gaze from the map "No excuses!"

Taking that as his cue to leave, Steve politely ended the impromptu meeting, watching Russell pick up his phone, presumably to discuss things further with the embattled CEO of the collapsing wholesaler.

He would need to get to Armstrong, and firm up his defences for the next few hours. Martin knew nothing of the wider plan, and was relying on blind trust in Steve, believing in the man, and his ability to bring something bigger and better in time, even if he couldn't see it.

Martin's office, 5 mins.

Firing off a text to Alison as he walked, knowing she would drop everything given such an instruction. The two of them would need to be a resolute first line of defence for the next 24 hours, following him into battle without question or reason.

Martin was sat at his desk, clearly debriefing Lucy on the events of the board meeting. Both seeing Steve, they smiled and the young brunette made her excuses and departed. Unsure whether she could be fully trusted yet, he chose to let her continue back to her desk, and not bring her to the inner circle, which was now completed with Alison's arrival.

"Thanks guys, appreciate it." taking up his regular pew on the corner of the table, above the two seated. "Administrators are being called into TWG today."

"Fuck!" Martin exclaimed

"Yeah, a bit quicker than we all expected." Steve checked the windows over his shoulder "It's going to get brutal."

"We're with you boss." inputted Martin keenly.

"Absolutely." Alison concurred.

"Russell wants solutions, the Germans or Thompsons. He needs to see some effort being put in there, I'm sure he will be putting in some calls himself today, so you need to beat him to it." He directed straight to a nodding Martin "Ali, can you support on that?"

"Of course, but not too much effort right?" She was certainly the savvier of the two, Steve chuckled.

"I'm sure there will be some huge hurdles to overcome, or their commercials will be way off." he continued "Which will leave FreshCo as the only lifeboat."

"He still won't take it will he?" Ali continued, clearly keeping pace, as Martin sat, squinting in concentration.

"Not likely," Steve confirmed. "but it gives it the best chance of success. I'll need to take that to him one on one."

Both Directors nodded in agreement, Martin slowly catching up with his counterpart, looking hopeful that he had caught onto the right end of the stick.

"TWG announcement will be out in a couple of hours, you'll both get heat for not having anything by then."

"We trust you." Martin leapt in, speaking for both parties once again.

"We do." Alison glared at him before turning to smile at Steve "As always, Steve."

Thanking them both, he agreed to meet with them again in a couple of hours. Leaving them to begin their simulated calls to the senior parties. Followed by a communicative briefing to the team gathered around the desks outside. The pretence should be enough cover for him should Russell wade in, his attitude had presented this risk to Steve, so mitigating it with his two trusted employees was the only move. Rarely did he have to defend during these games of political chess. With his guard down, the last few days had forced him to do it twice. This riled him.

Making his way down the carpeted stairs, greeting a number of nameless administrators as he did so, he stepped out into the brisk fresh air. Summoning his resolve to avoid a detour for a brief nicotine hit, he turned towards the IT block. Bolton would be given the hymn sheet, it was now going to be up to him if he sang the right tune.

11

. . . .

The Wholesale Group (TWG) have called in administrators, putting hundreds of jobs at risk.

Read more.

The news alert pinged on phones around the building, second and third waves of varying noises followed with the same information, as different outlets released their stories.

From the relative comfort of his desk, Steve cleared both notifications he had received at the top of his iPad and refreshed the share price page. Like the pictorial end of a linear mountain range, the decline was prominent. It had continued since early morning. Traders had already sniffed out the issues at TWG, the knock on effect to Russell's and they had placed their bets accordingly. Now it was paying off. Short sellers would see great gains in their portfolios, especially now the cat was pinging out of the bag. Market enthusiasts and slower long-game players may now begin looking at Russell's and dipping in. This would cause some volatility, smaller inclines and declines, however, they now all followed the same downward trend. Steve sat back and smiled.

"Yep!" Steve responded to the light knock at the door.

"I've booked you a room for tonight, Steve." Rachel smiled.

"Thank you, could you get me two nights?" returning his reserved smile.

Choosing to stay overnight locally was rare for Steve. However, with Sarah away, he saw no reason to make the lengthy round trip, especially as it was going to be a late one here.

"Dinner reservation for two?" Rachel asked jokingly, winking as she closed the door behind her.

Steve reached into the pocket of his bag and pulled out the phone. Stuffing it into his jacket pocket, he headed down the back staircase and out into the fields behind. Far from ideal, he knew he didn't have time to head out further. There may be some inquisitive looks to see the COO leaning on the boundary fence at the end of their land, but these were unprecedented times for the company.

He dialled the number a few paces from the fence.

"Niamh?"

"Steve, how is it going at your end?" Came the dulcet Irish tones "I guess you need to be quick"

"Could do with the fresh air to be honest." he chuckled "IT are prepared, Bolton saw sense in the end."

"Excellent, I'll keep waiting for the smoke." she smiled "The team can be there and link you up in a couple of days, as long as your lot are good to go. It will be very manual to start, but we can refine it once the data feeds are sorted."

"Perfect. They will be. We really appreciate it, Niamh." he confirmed. The conversation with Bolton earlier, whilst stressful, had yielded the required result.

"Great, commercials are ready and draft agreement is here with me now."

"Got my pen ready," Steve confirmed "finance boys won't be an issue."

"If you're sure, then I think we are on track."

"Short and sweet, Niamh." Steve sighed a relief that the plan was coming together.

"Not in my heels." she laughed.

Jones was nothing like Steve had expected, tales of her ruthlessness and dismissive attitude were proving to be wide of the mark. He enjoyed his dialogue with her, and could see a more trusted relationship being built once they were working closer together.

With that, Steve pushed the phone into the pocket behind his wallet, and briskly headed back to the main building. Closing in, he could see a figure walking from the back door, an older man, gaunt, in an ill fitting blue dress shirt and grey trousers. Stepping up his pace, he caught sight of the man climbing into an older Ford.

Jeffries.

Increasing his pace, he knew he wouldn't make it to the car in time to stop him, but it served to confirm his identity. Confusion ran through him, as he tried to work out why the dismissed Director had been sneaking through the rear door to that part of the building. Only Russell, and some of the HR and Payroll teams, were there. Surely a visit to the latter two would permit a main door entrance.

Reaching Russell's office, a few minutes before his required arrival time, he took a few deep breaths. His respect for the founder and CEO had grown in the weeks preceding this moment, however, if he was trying to pull something with Jeffries then the script for the next few minutes would be changing dramatically. He knocked, and entered.

"What we got then, Steven?" the jovial tone clearly used to mask something. Remaining sat behind his elegant desk, Steve pulled up a chair opposite.

"The Germans want too much. Asking for huge logistics costs, and not prepared to entertain a conversation to reduce pallet size." Steve paused.

"Less efficient." Russell allowed himself a wry smile.

"Exactly. No real surprises." He continued "Thompsons would be a huge risk, they aren't set up for it, so the delay alone ends us."

"And hybrid model as a bridge to something like Thompsons?"

"Not viable boss, Alan Thompson told me two years at best. We will be swimming belly up at that point."

Silence struck the old man. Cornered but with no fight, no route out. The two men looked at each other, Steve held his nerve to pull the trigger on him, he needed answers.

"What did Jeffries want?"

The blunt delivery gave Russell little room for manoeuvre. His eyes hinting to Steve that what was coming wasn't going to be the full story.

"I wanted to sound him out. On the options. Pretty much echoed what you just said." trying to shrug it off his shoulders.

Steve considered how hard to push on this, without anything further from the founder, he would have to take the risk. Why hadn't he been involved in this sounding out? Was the deal rumbled? Was Jeffries in receipt of details of his own execution? Doubting himself, the elongated pause became increasingly awkward.

"Did you bump into him outside?" He nervously asked.

"Sadly not, just saw him leaving."

"Sorry, Steve, please don't think I don't trust your judgment or that I think you're lying." the old man crumbled.

"It's fine John, you've been close for years." Steve stared Russell down, desperate to read him. "I get it."

"We are left with this hybrid model, and a ticking time bomb then?" Moving to change the subject.

Steve now stood, and began pacing to the window.

"Steve?" Russell confused by the lack of response.

Staring out the window, events flashed through his mind. Everything that had led to this point. The strings he had been pulled, the rungs he had climbed.

"FreshCo." he delivered, facing the window.

"What?" Came the response, feigning a lack of hearing.

"FreshCo." Steve turned, steely eyed, chest puffed.

"No fucking chance." Russell waved his hand in the air "Go back to the Thompsons. Tell you what, I'll ring Alan, talk some sense into him."

Just as Russell had lifted his phone from his pocket, Steve was leaning over the desk. Pushing the founders hand down to the desk, adding pressure against the device. He felt the old mans bones creaking against the metal casing.

"No". he eyeballed him.

"What the fuck do you think you're doing?" shocked Russell, his expression draining colour.

Steve remained standing over the older man, saying nothing. Eventually he relieved the pressure on his hand, which he retracted instantly, trying to shake the bones back into place. The phone was moved to the edge nearest the imposing COO.

"Don't make this an issue, John." finally he spoke.

"What the fuck? Have you lost the fucking plot?" Russell demanded. Still lacking colour and strength. This was flight not fight.

Steve picked up the phone, and placed it on the large expansive table. Well out of Russell's reach, he wouldn't dare to stand against him.

"I'm going to give you two clear options, John." Steve returned over the desk, his chest and shoulders stood proud, hands taking root in his pockets.

"You don't give me ultimatums Steve, remember your place here. This is my business." Pushing his finger into the desk in defiance.

"A business you've taken to a cliff edge, you had chances to avoid this. And now, the one solution we have, you're dismissing out of stubbornness. Spite."

"They are vultures Steve. They will destroy everything I've built. We will survive without them, I promise you that." his vehement words failed to have the physical back up, as he slumped back in his chair.

"For how long. 6 months if you're lucky. The share price is in the toilet John. That's on you." his right index finger pointing over the desk, before returning swiftly to his pocket.

"So we sell our soul? No, they will tear us apart, this business won't exist in 6 months. I won't sign a deal with them. Not a chance."

"No, you won't." letting it linger, Steve watched the realisation dawn on Russell's face. They wouldn't sign with him either.

"But you will. You'll sell everyone in this fucking business down the river. Of course you would."

"You're done for John. Investors are crawling all over us. Millions off the value. They are baying for blood."

The old man looked out the window, he knew the truth in this statement. Over the last few hours, the phone that now sat meters away from him, had not left his ear. Calls from the disgruntled foreign investors, an angry Chairman who was acting as a conduit to the same group, adding to the pressure. Silence fell upon the room once more.

"Walk away quietly John" Steve softened to an urge, dropping his demanding tone. "Leave with your head held high. You told me you wanted to retire. Do it."

No response came from Russell's direction.

"We will look after you financially, I give you my word."

"and if I don't?" the fair headed man spat, still unable to make eye contact.

"Then the wolves will get you John. That's not how you should leave everything you created." there was a candor to his words which caused Russell to turn towards him.

"I should have seen this coming. This is why you talked me out of retiring before. You wanted the blood to be on my hands."

"TWG have been struggling for.."

"Not that, none of that. You. I should have seen this coming, from you." Dejected but not out yet, the last remaining fight being spat towards the aggressor.

"Mark tried to warn me, that's why he was here. Little did either of us know you had it all worked out."

Stewing, the old man wrangled, like a broken Jekyll and Hyde, visibly twisting, and turning in his own head. It had not been easy for Steve to watch. Remorse waved through his insides, he deserved a respectful exit, but he was making it increasingly hard for himself. He had never expected it to feel like this.

"You win."

"Thank you, John." he attempted to reconcile, or at least pay deference to the difficult decision he had made. Showing humility was not Steve's strong point, but in this moment, it took no effort at all.

"Fuck you, Steve!" throwing his head back, trying to control his visible emotion.

Decades building this business. Fighting, single handedly at times, to make it a success. Reaching heady heights before the cracks had started to appear, and the empire began to crumble. The young pretender now stood in his office, overthrowing him, using his own values and morals against him, made him sick to the pit of his stomach. However, as the final words left his mouth, he felt a calmness over him. Colour slowly returned to his cheeks, as he bought himself back to the desk.

"I just hope you know what you're doing." he continued. All fight had left him, resignation reigned. "Mark was right about that, you are smarter than the lot of us. But have you got the balls Bellingham?"

****

Niamh Jones sat and looked at the message.

White smoke.

Clearly, Bellingham had delivered on his promise. With the stubborn bull out of the way, things could progress.

Taking to her feet, she crossed her expansive eighth floor office, over looking the exposed central core of the building. From the glass surrounds of the room, she could see all the way to the ground floor entrance. Constant flurrying of bee-like workers in and out of the lift, going about their set routines. Fetching, carrying, meeting, delivering, it was all the same. Monotonous operatives, living off the measly sums of money they were dished out every month.

The exposed metal framework, and walls of toughened glass, segmented the floors below. Each visible row of desks, the same as those below. Here she stood, as queen of the colony, as indistinguishable drones busied themselves below. She had detested her time on the lower levels. Playing the political game left a nasty taste in her mouth, even now. Now she wielded the power she deserved, and could take things in the direction she saw fit.

Exiting her room onto the expansive floor, a small bank of desks in the middle housed the group PAs. The brightest of this year's graduate intake, they would go on to do senior roles quickly, a model that had worked well. Opposite her, however, could not have been more contrasting. Group level Directors' offices, home to wooden desks and ornately framed pictures. Their inhabitants would be at home with the recently dispatched Russell. Of a generation past. However, these positions were all but inherited, hand me downs, and deals over private school handshakes.

She ignored the lot, choosing to spend time with progressive people not afraid of change and challenge. Scanning her ID card through the double doors and striding down one flight of stairs, before scanning herself again into the next floor. Entering the only room on the floor, and one of few in the building, that was completely private. Soundproofed panels, and increased digital security, these rooms were normally left fallow, reserved for sensitive HR issues.

Years ago, she would never have been able to book these out for a day, let alone the time she had now. No questions asked, the space had been handed over to her for nigh on six months. Weeks before the planted Kingsland/Russell's story. Equipment and resource had been in abundance.

Inside, the climate controlled room was a perfect working temperature. She had handed over creative control of the interior to her trusted fixer, and she had not let her down. The small, but effective, team inside looked cheerful and happy, empty branded coffee cups adorned the desks and breakout space. Brightly coloured scrawls covered large flip chart sheets stuck to the thick panelled walls.

"How's everyone doing in here? Got what you need?" She announced her arrival.

She was a frequent visitor to the room, but still caused a shockwave when she arrived. Headphones were quickly removed, and attention turned to the sharp-suited, high heeled CEO. Polite and positive nods and noises spread throughout, before Ellie Ash stepped forward.

"Everything is going really well, I think we are a step ahead of the plan." she angled towards the professionally developed GANNT chart covering almost one side of the office, as she approached Niamh.

"Excellent, I shouldn't be surprised." greeting her warmly with a continental double kiss. "Tell me more. We've got the amber light from Russell's now. John will be retiring, and Steve Bellingham taking over. Just need some time to let that become official."

"Great news!" a smile of pride crossed Ellie's face "well Chris and Scott have found a way of taking some CSV data into the forecasting system."

Niamh knew enough of the technical detail to keep pace with the vibrant young individuals, as they outlined their plans to take raw sales information from the till system of the convenience store chain and convert it into their system's language. Something that would speed up the process, and keep them all more accurate.

Further updates on vehicle sourcing, logistics databases, and temporary stock picking staff all came flooding through as the key individuals stood around the carefully developed plan. Nothing was going to be left to chance. Meticulous planning and attention to detail were cliched, buzz words around this building, but there was no better exponent of these arts than the lady from Enniskillen.

Every element pleased Jones, as she thanked the relevant department experts, she called Ellie to one side. Young, passionate, and no particular job title beyond "Special Projects", she was a shining light, someone who would go on to great roles very soon. Niamh had earmarked her for one piece in particular.

"El, I want you to lead things in Stevenage."

"Seriously? Wow, I thought Operations or Trading would put someone in, that's what we planned."

"Absolutely, once the package is through the group exec tonight, we will begin getting the team together, but I want you to know your name is at the top of that list." She watched as the grin of pride washed across the young project manager.

"I'd be, well I'd be honoured, if that's the right thing to say?" She giggled.

"You deserve it, you've done an incredible job here, the detail, the passion, the delivery. It's exceptional Ellie."

With that, she left the glowing young woman to gather herself, and get her team back to their tasks. Niamh cleared the security doors back to the eighth floor, stopping in the centre console desks to address the group PAs.

"Can you get the gents together immediately for me please? In my office."

"Certainly Mrs Jones." came the professional reply from her right.

Back in her office, she gathered her notes and prepared to dazzle the four gentlemen that would be meandering their way over any time soon. Huffing and puffing at being summoned at such a time on a Monday, but also at having to walk the distance, she sniggered.

The Group Executive Committee comprised of the overseeing eyes of the entire business, and its various sub entities. She had smashed her way into this group in a couple of years, and confounded those around her. What she was about to deliver would take this to a whole new level. Rarely would a CEO establish such a package without breathing word of it, these things would normally be subject to strategic scrutiny at many levels. Whilst she had done nothing against the unwritten rulebook, this was not standard procedure, and would ruffle the feathers of the old boys.

Men, and indeed many women, in this world which they existed responded only to one master. Money. Whether through direct remuneration, investment, or a maturity of an asset. The common tongue was clear. Her sole argument would be enough, she saw no reason to think otherwise. Explaining to them, the impact to their wallets, and in particular, their share options, would see it over the line.

****

Steve packed his phone away in the bottom of the bag. She continued to impress him. She seemed to command her business, taking no prisoners. Somehow pushing through a huge strategic move in such short time, overcoming years of challenges, and made it look easy. He sat back in his chair and checked the time on his watch. It was getting late, and so many of the office teams had departed. Only a small crew kept on with Martin to begin some of the work required for their link up. Selecting just a few that could be trusted, even though it wasn't as much a risk now if things began to leak.

With the share price ending at its lowest ever for the company, rumours were already spreading about John Russell's future. Steve took a moment to soak it in. Allowing his mind to drift, and considered what type of CEO he would be. All the time, and energy, spent on getting so close to that point, he had rarely sat to consider what it would look like, what it would feel like. He looked around and felt nothing.

Picking up the phone, he answered the Chairman's call. Expecting it to be on time, as he always was. The short shrift delivery was also no revelation. Delivering the news of Russell's intention to retire, and asking Steve to hold the fort as Interim CEO, almost delivered in one breath. John had done his piece and informed him of the intention to move to FreshCo's supply, and that given Steve's involvement in bringing the deal to life, he should be asked to run it to completion. Plans would now be made to announce the transition to the city first thing tomorrow, with the hope of resurrecting the share price, and in turn raising the value of the company back to a more reasonable level.

Barely ten minutes had passed when the call ended. Like a whirlwind, his plans for the last few months, his ambitions for the last few years were being realised. He grabbed his bag, nodded at himself with pride and made his way to the car.

The quietness of the corridor was poles apart from earlier in the day, a buzz of shock and rumour. Distressed older staff, panicking at the potential downfall of the business they had known all their lives. Mags and her husband had crossed paths outside his office, and were close to consoling each other. He smiled as he realised the positive message he could deliver in the morning, winning the hearts and minds across the staff.

His positivity grew by the time he reached the hotel, for the second time in a few days he was scanning himself into a large, spacious hotel room. Throwing his items down. He opened the mini bar, and pulled out a can of lager, cracking it open, sitting on the bed and flicking off his shoes so they were strewn on the floor. Leaning back on his elbows, he unbuckled his belt and relaxed. Pride waved through him. Many would not agree with how he got here, but he had.

All of a sudden, there was a knock at the door.

"Room Service."

Knowing he hadn't ordered anything, he ignored it.

"Room Service for Mr Bellingham."

Pulling his trousers together, he made his way over and peaked through the peep hole. Grinning widely, he opened the door, as she entered, flowing golden locks, and familiar perfume. A bottle of Champagne in one hand, and two glasses in the other.

12

. . . .

Steve woke to the buzz of his phone, luckily left charging next to the hotel room bed. He rolled over and looked at Rachel, she was slowly stirring. His head a little fuzzy.

"Morning." he looked at her, kissing her on the forehead as he got up and headed to the shower.

She slowly stirred, wrapping the bed sheet around her, and sitting up in bed. Her blonde hair spread out wide across the large white pillows, smiling cutely as Steve returned, towel around his waist.

"I need to get ready." as much as he wished he didn't.

"Big day." she returned, gathering the sheet around her, heading to the shower "Chief Executive Bellingham."

Preening his hair in the mirror, he saw his own reaction. A slight wince, he must have let it out over the Champagne bottle. Not that there would be major repercussions, he just rarely let his guard down in such a way.

Hearing the water flowing in the shower, he briskly buttoned up his clean white shirt, and dipped into the bottom of his bag. The screen denoted a host of missed calls and messages. His heart thumped in his chest.

Staring intently at the phone, he cycled through the missed calls, all of which from the contact number he never saved. They never called. The messages gave more insight. Single word denotations. What had he missed? Eventually he got to the last message.

Disappointing. Had to hear through other parties. Discuss in morning.

"Multiple phones for multiple girls?" came the voice in his ear, still damp arms wrapped around his broad shoulders. "Clearly upset one of them."

She kissed him on the ear, before heading over to the bed to get herself dressed, leaving him in shock.

"Just work stuff, promise." he attempted to pass off.

"It's fine, I know how this works." she dismissed.

Steve hurried back a message, he would have to call on the way in to the office. It had worked when he made contact with Niamh, there was no reason why it wouldn't work now.

Walking over to the bed, in his fresh shirt and pants, he sat on Rachels side of the bed, watching her put on a fine layer of make up from her large handbag.

"I'll need to go home and get my stuff, so might be a few minutes late."

"Look, about last night." Steve ignored.

"I know how this works, I won't get hurt." she pouted into the small mirror.

"No, I mean about what I told you."

"About the new job? Oh come on. I'd need to know today anyway." she continued, Steve relaxed somewhat "And the bonus, well that's private anyway!"

Packing up her items into the handbag, she finally looked at Steve. Calculations were crunching in his mind, he had said something about money. Pulling through his fuzzy memories from the night, he couldn't place what he had said.

"Unless of course you want to buy me something nice?" she leant in, young slender arms wrapping around his arm. Her lips softly kissing his shoulder.

Steve pulled away, unable to develop the mental clarity for an answer, worried he would inadvertently spill more to this beautiful young woman dressing herself next to him.

"Lets see about that." was all he could muster. Not wanting to lose what he had with her.

"Always wanted a sugar daddy." she chuckled, putting on her shoes and standing, bag in hand ready to leave the room. "See you in a couple of hours Mr CEO."

Kissing him longingly on the lips, she left the hotel room, the heavy clunk of the door preceding all but silence in the room. He sat, gathering his thoughts as the rhythmic dripping of the shower head continued in the background.

Pulling the phone from his pocket, he noticed a response from the private number. Not surprising, these people seemed to work every hour. He dialled the number.

"We were disappointed not to hear from you last night." came the voice, barely a single ring later.

"Got a bit tied up, sorry." rarely forced to apologise, but given the set up here, he had no choice.

"Yes, she's a lovely girl Steve, but you need to be careful."

Shockwaves burst through his body, like electric current running through his arms. The adrenaline clearing any residual haze from his mind, as he grabbled with what had been thrown at him. Struggling to comprehend how the nameless, faceless, voice knew about his actions of last night.

"Understood." his voice shook.

"Steve, consider this your one and only warning. You know the terms of this deal. Do your part."

With that, the line went dead. Steve shut off the phone and placed it next to him before running his fingers through his hair. His breath was short, and chest tight with fear. He frantically looked around the room for some sort of signal as to how they knew Rachel had been here. As if he was expecting to find a camera or recording device, he paced the room. Spotting his paling expression in the mirror, he attempted to pull that forward, only to reveal the same mottled beige wallpaper that covered the entire room.

Hurriedly, he put on his the rest of his designer workwear. Shoving the phone into his pocket, convincing himself he needed to be closer to that today than it languishing, locked away in the bottom of his bag. Shoving both plastic room keys into his other pocket he made his way out of the room, a cursory leaving glance to make sure he hadn't left anything important before likely returning tonight.

Making his way back through the ivy archway towards reception, he noted the Christmas lights, they hadn't struck him on Friday, but in the cold, frosty, white morning, they took more prominence. The reception area itself was awash with gaudily decorated fake trees, and bright lighting. Wrapped boxes, with torn edges, sat under the stand which held the largest tree at a slight angle. Desperate last adverts dotted around the walls, urging people to eat their Christmas or Boxing Day dinner in the hotel, for extortionate prices. With only a few days to go, he wondered if there were going to be many takers.

Clearly he was so lost in the events of the last few months, only the functional business of Christmas had been addressed. Most of that work actually happening in the tail end of the summer. Crunching across the courtyard gravel, he realised, he had not got anything yet for his wife. She was still holed up at her parents house, but due to return any day now.

Promising himself he would sort that out the next few days, he scribbled a note on his notebook resting in the passenger seat of the car, and started the engine.

"Could spell the end really." came the voice from the radio. Ending a statement clearly already diving into yesterday's dealings.

"I wouldn't be surprised, Iz, they need to move quick over the next couple of days, but their silence just doesn't bode well."

Steve notched the volume up from his steering wheel as he turned out of his space, before rolling over the loose stone surface and turning out onto the main road. Listening to the negativity, and impending doom, surrounding his own company, the one he was now going to lead, was entertaining. Causing him a wry chuckle, as he floored his right foot.

****

Her heels clicked against the pavement as she headed towards the office steps, taking sips from her reusable Costa cup as she walked. She half jogged up the few steps that lead to the wide front entrance of the office complex, choosing as she always did, the right hand revolving door. An acknowledging smile from the security guard, and those at reception, who despite her position, still glanced at her ID pass hanging from the lanyard around her neck.

Sipping the remaining drops of coffee from her cup, she watched as the glass lift approached from the floors above. Eventually the doors opening in front of her, and she stepped in, alone. Riding up to the top floor of the building took only a few seconds, but allowed her to soak in the surrounding area as she climbed. From the top, the views over the hills in the distance on a clear morning like this, reminded her of home, only a few miles away.

After greeting the keen graduates already furiously typing away on the central desk, she took a seat in her large office. Fishing out a gold lipstick holder from her handbag now sat on the desk, she flipped open the lid and, using the concealed mirror, touched up any areas that the coffee cup had disturbed on the journey in.

She knew the team housed on the floor below were already powering through the final details of the Russell's plan. Her phone had buzzed a few short emails detailing their progress since the early hours. Knowing that Ellie would be giving it every last effort gave her great comfort. Later today she would be making her way down to Stevenage with a handful of her team to begin the transition work. Niamh herself would go, but only once the groundwork was laid, and the timing was right.

With the elder statesmen placated yesterday evening, this morning's conference call across the wider operational board of Directors would certainly go much smoother. Only a few minutes to go until she dialled into it, she checked her notes, beautifully written in her small leather book. Plans that had been rumbling around varying corners, were now being bought into the light.

Her twin prong approach had worked well so far. Only key Directors, who mostly reported to her, were briefed, and only on the information vital to the plan. Some knew more than others, but they were trustworthy individuals, and had kept their end of the bargain. Many knew nothing. Today's call would address this completely.

"Good morning everyone, thank you for dialling in, we are waiting on two more people before I hand over to Niamh." came the familiar voice of Zak, the bright young PA sat just outside Niamh's eye line.

Two beeps later and Zak passed the call over to Niamh to begin. A seamless transition, managed many times over.

"Good morning ladies and gentlemen, I'm going to keep this brief." she announced "You will have seen the news yesterday regarding TWG's collapse."

An expert orator in these occasions, a well timed pause would allow the less well-versed individuals to conduct a swift Google search.

"Their collapse leaves thousands of smaller convenience stores on a ticking time bomb. Stock, especially fresh, will be drained fast. Now, TWG's administrators are due to confirm this morning that they will oversee the dispatch of all remaining stocks over the remainder of the week, and into next. However, I'm sure you can all imagine how well that's going to go down."

She paused for laughter, the shop facing representatives chuckling the loudest.

"Whilst the pond is worth fishing in, we are already hearing of independents and smaller chains working through the night to establish new supply deals today, and fair play to them, speed and agility will always be their modus operandi. Our opportunity lies within the largest fish in that rapidly draining pond."

A further pause, letting the virtual room catch up. Russell's should be on everyones mind by now, she concluded.

"Our opportunity lies in utilising our unique supply chain, our stellar brand, and our phenomenal teams to do something spectacular. That is why I am delighted today, to announce, we will soon commence supplying Russell's Retail through our existing depot network."

A couple of sharp intakes of breath from the uninitiated, but nothing that would disrupt the call.

"Now, for some of you, that will be a massive surprise, and I want to apologise to you now, personally, for having kept you in the dark until this point. This was not intentional. This is not how I like to work. I hope you can understand, as is sometimes the case, we needed to work behind close doors, to protect both our shareholders, and theirs."

She shouldn't have to explain herself, but it played into her personal style.

"The sensitivity of this deal is huge. As I'm sure you'll see later this morning when we officially announce. I want to thank those of you who were involved in the recent discussions, for your candor, but also for your confidentiality. I understand how difficult it has been at times. Now, we will brief this to the wider business at 10am, as will the team at Russell's, with press releases due out any moment now."

She looked for a thumbs up from the central desk.

"Finally, their announcement will include the news that John Russell will be standing down with immediate effect as Russell's Chief Executive Officer. I have passed my best wishes to John on behalf of the business, and also to Steve Bellingham who will be stepping up as Interim CEO."

A few hushed murmurs of shock.

"At this point, I am not going to take any questions. Any queries relating directly to the supply deal can be picked up with Ellie Ash, who is also on the call, and will be leading the relationship with Russell's."

With that, she wrapped up the call. No doubt leaving Ellie to field a barrage of them. Glancing at her mobile, Niamh declined the only one she had expected to come straight to her. That could wait, and would get dealt with in time. Logging in, she flicked straight to, and then tapped, the share price app.

****

"Thank you for all coming at short notice". Russell stood as he spoke, a slight crackle in his voice. He appeared to have aged dramatically overnight. "I'm not going to beat around the bush here. Last night, I expressed my desire to step down as Chief Executive."

A flurry of shot glances. Everyone looking for reactions, or more importantly, non-reactions. Eventually, eyes settled on Steve. Keeping his gaze straight and true on the older man.

"The timing isn't great, but given the challenges we face, and a few impending changes, it is the right decision for me, and for the company."

He hung his head, hands in his pockets, a pose he had never briefed them from before, as he leant on the windowsill of his vast office.

"I've informed the non-execs, and they have unanimously agreed that Steve will step in as Interim CEO whilst a full, and thorough, recruitment process is undertaken."

All eyes were on Steve, he remained unmoved, until the very end. A respectful nod, and feigned humble smile, preceded a mouthed thanks to the outgoing leader.

"Steve, I assume you would like to brief on the next piece?" Clearly John was unable to bring himself to deliver the news to the gathering of Directors.

"Of course, John," he cleared his throat "it is my honour and privilege to be asked to lead this business for the interim period. Words are not enough to give thanks to everything John has done for this business. In time, we will find our way of giving him the send off he so richly deserves."

Nods and smiles spread around the room.

"We face the greatest of challenges right here and now. The TWG news has hit us all hard, and there are a lot of worried people out there." Waving his hand towards the door. "Now, many of you will not agree with what I'm about to announce, but I need you to consider the responsibility we all have to secure the future of what John has created."

John coughed. Whilst nobody else in the room reacted, it was clear to Steve that his empty words were suffocating him. He cast a forlorn look.

"Thanks to the excellent work of Alison and Martin over the last few days, we have managed to secure a supply deal with FreshCo. This will be phased in alongside the remainder of TWG stock."

Pausing, expecting a positive buzz through the room, he was disappointed. Regaining his composure he continued.

"They will be sending a small team down over the next few days to begin the linking up of systems, and supporting both the IT, and Trading departments, through this tricky time. The press release is…" checking his watch "going out now, and we will brief the office at ten. John and I both need to see you to be fully on board with both."

Russell did little conceal his contorted, uncomfortable, face.

"Well, as Steve said, everyone in the canteen at ten please, we can pick up from there. Thanks guys."

As the gathering departed, in small groups and pairs, each of them discussed their varying levels of shock and surprise. Steve waited until everyone had left, including a lingering Phil Bolton, and turned to address Russell.

"Steve," he began, now staring out the window "You will get my best performance down there, but right now, the last thing I want to do is see your face, let alone share small talk."

Not wanting to engage, Steve left. Bitterness and resentment had clearly spread through him over the course of the evening.

Checking his phone as he walked, wading through a number of news report notifications and business updates, he dived in to check out the share prices.

As expected, the announcements had clearly excited both the market gamblers, and long term strategic investors. The price was climbing strongly, compounded by the low base, the visuals of the high percentage increases, served to draw more money into the stock. In turn, highlighting them on the varying comparison tables, and high performance shares. A virtuous cycle which eradicated any frustration Steve had with the previous leader.

"She's here." Came the voice from behind the half open door.

Rachel had seen him staring into his phone, flicking through various menus and details on the share dealings when the notification of Ellie's arrival had dropped on her screen.

"Thank you, Rachel." He smiled around the corner, leaving her with a little wink.

Ellie Ash was sat in the dingy reception area. The worn blue chairs not the most guest friendly, but now a couple of the fluorescent box lights had begun to flicker. An atrium beginning to resemble the waiting room from a horror movie mortuary.

"Ellie?" Steve warmly greeted.

"Mr Bellingham." Came the confident response.

"Steve, please." He shook her hand. "Let's get you set up shall we?"

Leading the young executive through the creaking cheapness of the company headquarters, he felt a sense of embarrassment. He'd seen pictures of the FreshCo offices, and their bright splendour, in the various trade magazines. One day, he should be there, he considered, but for now, he was leading one of their up and coming stars, through his damp ridden concrete clad eyesore.

Once her new office had been established, she and Steve made their way up to his office, discussing as they walked.

"Desks are being set up in IT, and Trading for your team's arrival, and Martin will give you a tour in a bit, but is there anything else you need right now?"

"No, no, this is great. The majority of the team are on their way down now. Most of them should arrive today."

"OK, this is Rachel, she's my wonderful PA, you need anything at all, just ask her."

The two warmly greeted each other, Rachel doing her very best to keep her professional front, despite a little blush with the gushing praise.

"I need to nip out for half hour," Steve looked at Rachel to confirm the private space in his diary, she acknowledged with a smiling nod, "Martin will be up in a few minutes."

"That's great, thank you, Steve."

Checking his watch as he entered his office, he knew it would be a bit tight, especially to prepare for the barrage of questions he would receive in a little over thirty minutes. He knew he couldn't trust Russell to be exact on message, and so, resolved to make this as quick as possible. Grabbing his bag and keys, he darted down the back stairs and into the driver's seat of the car.

As he pulled away the barriers, he kept one hand on the steering wheel, and the other inside his leather back, unzipping and grabbing the secondary phone. Glancing between the phone and the road ahead, he dialled the number from the text messages, mentally kicking himself for not deleting them. Swiftly he pulled into a residential area off the roundabout into town, and parked the car, keeping the ignition on.

"Steve."

"Morning, I don't have long."

"No, I know. We won't hold you up. Your positions are strong as of this morning. Funds will be distributed in the normal way, and we will continue with the current strategy unless you advise us otherwise."

"OK." Steve agreed, a mix of unease and uncertainty. The mysterious individual clearly aware of his plans for the day.

"We are projecting gains to continue through the next couple of weeks, and will manage accordingly. That will see us on a stable footing into the New Year."

"Agreed."

"At which point we will restrict activity. Let the dust settle for a while so to speak. Unless of course."

The imposing voice paused, longer than was comfortable, Steve's queasy feeling continued through to his stomach.

"Smooth sailing from January." Steve interrupted.

"Unless of course, there are any, unforeseen circumstances." A further, shorter pause on the line. "You won't hear from us until the New Year, Steve."

"Right. OK. Understood."

"Oh, and Merry Christmas."

13

"I'll need to run that one past Niamh." repeated Ellie.

Steve huffed into his notes, with a tilted head, and closed his eyes. Placing his pen down on the large table, he rubbed the stubble around his cheeks and down to his chin, taking a deep breath through his nose as he did so.

During the first board meeting under Steve's control, she had already cemented her position. Now, by the third, she was becoming insufferable. He hadn't even agreed to her sitting in on such gatherings verbally, but when he had challenged Niamh Jones, she quoted verbatim, a deeply buried clause in the final contract. Her eyes and ears on every decision.

He glanced around the room, looking for support, and nothing was forthcoming.

"It's purely operational, Ellie." Speaking through his fingers.

"But will impact delivery volumes and schedules." She countered, calmly.

"Tell you what Ellie, I'll pick this up with Niamh. Let's move on."

Weeks had passed since Steve had last exploded in an expletive laden rant, and he was having to control every will in his body to not do so now. This youngster was pulling every string in the puppet show. He could not abide it for much longer.

Dismissing the meeting with a growled conclusion, hung heads quietly left the room. Leaving him sat, alone, at the large oval table. Considering his next moves, he felt he was swimming the channel in a straight jacket at the moment. Niamh was to blame, and he knew it. She had manipulated the situation to her advantage, and now she had remote control of every move and decision.

Powering the palms of both hands into the table, he caused the glass bottles in the centre to chime as he stood. Like a boxer's bell, he was ready for this fight.

Striding up his stairs, ignoring all that stood in his way, he entered his office and slammed the door. Phone in hand he dialled the number for the FreshCo CEO. It was unlikely she would answer, but he needed to try.

As expected, the line was engaged, no doubt was in Steve's mind as to who she was talking to. A knock at the door was all that stopped him storming down the corridor to confront her.

"Room service." came the delicate voice, hardly above a whisper.

Normally, Rachel's flirty entrance would bring a smile to his face. For weeks they had met at the regular hotel, sharing copious bottles of Champagne. He was still wildly attracted to her, watching her figure as she entered the room, and closed the door. However, as she feigned a catwalk stride over to him, his mind was elsewhere, and could hardly raise a smile for her.

"Grumpy this morning I see." She pushed him playfully back in his chair. "I missed you this weekend."

"Not now, Rach." He retracted.

She stepped back, offended by the rejection.

"Martin and Alison both want time with you today." She spoke coldly.

Both were looking for their reward for supporting Steve to the point he was in today, beyond the personal Christmas bonus cheques, that only they had received. They had equally risked a great deal in pulling off the plan, and now wanted a shot to fill the vacuum created by his elevation. Tensions were becoming evident between the pair.

"Tomorrow. First thing."

"Right. Still need the room for this week?"

"Yeah, please." He rubbed his brow, before sitting back and watching her walk towards the door. "But find somewhere new."

He couldn't see, but she smiled as she left. Stress over the swirling events was beginning to consume him, hardly returning him to Sarah during the week, he chose to remain in fully serviced comfort. His nightly visitor was also a big factor in his decision. Passing it off to his wife as a need to stabilise the business through the challenging times, she had no reason to question it, but yet she did.

She had almost caught him making out the sizeable cheques to his trusted pair, entering the kitchen just as he was signing them. His frantic reaction and hiding of the personal chequebook had only fuelled the flames with Sarah. Already harbouring a growing distrust of her life partner, she was now beginning to question their financial position.

Alongside the secretive five digit cheques he was now making out to his closest colleagues, she had spotted a number of new watches, and stationery items appearing in his collections. Nothing had been completed through their limited joint account, only through his personal one, and no sign of a receipt could be found around the house. All of which culminating in a blazing row to start the year.

"I think he was going to come find you." came the mumbled female voice from the other side of the door.

"Is he in?" He recognised the voice immediately as Ellie.

"Not now!" he bellowed sternly.

"Steve. About earlier." Ellie positioned herself through a crack in the door, her confidence growing as she spent time around the building.

He rocked back, swept his hair, and leaned forward into the desk on his elbows.

"You understand this is my office right?"

"Sorry, Steve, I just wanted to deal with this, I don't like this situation." She slipped further in, closing the door by gently leaning back on it.

"Then you shouldn't have agreed to be her little spy! Coming down here and meddling in everything we need to do!"

His phone buzzed.

"Ah there she is, must be to tell me off. Leave, please."

Ellie left as quietly as she entered, as Steve answered the call.

"Niamh, we need to chat about this." He barraged.

"Morning to you too, Steve." Her calming tone, taking the sting out of his barb.

"She's getting too involved, getting her fingers into everything. I'm having to field complaints daily about her information requests. HR, IT, Finance. The lot."

"Steve, you know why she's there." calmer, and slower now.

"Of course I fucking do, but seriously, does she need to be in all of it?"

"Yes." She paused. "If it impacts on us."

Exasperation crackled down the line.

"Given what we have had to endure the last few weeks, Steve, I understand that this seems like an invasion. You know that it's only for the benefit of both of us in the long run."

Steve grudgingly conceded, ending the call like a moody teenager who had just been proved wrong. His temper was getting shorter, clouding his judgement, and slowing his reactions. Frustration at the range of challenges he was embroiled in, he was acting out of sorts. Foggy thinking and poor decision making was seeing him stumble.

He knew deep down there was nothing he could do about the intrusions. The 'open book' stipulation in a watertight contract, that had been hurriedly signed, had him over a barrel. At first, it had seemed fairly innocuous. Coming to light as Ellie had started rifling through pricing strategies, and promotional plans. The company CFO had taken it upon himself to re-read the contract and bought it to Steve's attention.

Expensively outsourced solicitors also confirmed the predicament. Despite trying to placate him, assuring him of the non-disclosure elements, this had little effect. Within days she was diving deeper and deeper into the company databases.

To their credit, FreshCo had some immensely talented people who were running rings around the IT guys, fixing issues that had been in the systems for years, in a matter of days. The embarrassment this had caused Bolton, had been very enjoyable.

Fixes such as these, as well as a strong relationship with Martin's trading team had gone a long way in masking Ellie's activities. Steve knew he needed to remind himself of the bigger picture more often, without this deal they would have been sunk without trace, he would be having to start over somewhere new, or worse, jobless. As it stood, he was awaiting his confirmation as permanent CEO, and now had access to a multi-million pound bank balance.

****

She knew she could have sent one of the multiple PAs out to stand in this queue, but she had needed the space. Bellingham was becoming a thorn in her side.

"Soya Cappuccino to go please."

He was clearly distracted. No doubt trying to balance his growing list of sordid secrets. This was impacting on Ellie, and the rest of the FreshCo team stitching up the gaping holes in that wretched building.

Regret had never crossed her mind, the deal had been easier to land in her own company than she had anticipated. Telling herself it was down to her attitude, that a pessimist is never disappointed, but the truth was, her meticulous planning, and well managed relationships had seen it sail through. FreshCo shares had strengthened on the back of this, and was reflected in the improving mood of the Directors around her.

She grabbed her eco-friendly cup from the end of the counter, and exited, turning the wrong way. Walking around the side of the coffee shop, she crossed the road, and into the small park. The air brisk and cold, her drink steamed up into the clear sky. With her other hand, she grabbed the mobile from the inside of her pinstripe blazer.

She typed a brief message, pressed send, and sipped her coffee.

****

"I've made my decision." Steve concluded.

"Glad I could help," JT smiled. "Now, let's talk about you."

"What about me?" A snorted chuckle, desperate to come across calm and relaxed.

"I know it's not been an easy few weeks, just know that I'm here to help you however I can." She continued.

"Thanks Jane, that really means a lot."

"I can't shake the feeling we've got a few skeletons in the cupboard. Anything we need to be prepared for?"

Her reference to the growing pile of bodies on Steve's path to the summit, was not lost on him. They were necessary, but presented a greater risk, the higher he got. JT was savvy enough to recognise that not all of these bodies were there through natural causes.

"We don't need to talk about it now, but if there is anything I need to prepare, I will."

"What would I do without you?" He forced a smile.

"That's better, now, it's getting late, shall we call it a day?"

The day had flown, their regular catch up meeting having to be moved to the end of the day to accommodate the growing demands of his new role. JT's calming influence had helped, in small part, to get him out of his earlier stupor.

"Absolutely."

"Hotel again?" She asked, as they walked down the stairs to the exit.

"Yeah, building works overrunning."

"Ah I see." Disinterested, regardless of the brazen lie. "Catch you in the morning."

Steve fell into the driver's seat, drained, and sat there for a moment. He fired off a short factual text to Sarah, advising her of his next steps, before turning the ignition and moving the car towards the gate.

Radio Classic did its part in soothing his racing mind a little, with only a few minutes drive to the hotel, it also gave him time to gather his thoughts. The bodies could hurt him, but overthinking their presence would do more damage, recent days had proved this. There was only one body on his mind as he pulled into the hotel car park. Far more industrial than his previous choice, a standard city centre multi-storey block, that lacked a character. A standard chain, where upon waking up, you could be anywhere in the world. Moving hotel had been necessity after being rumbled before Christmas.

Surprisingly, he found he had already checked in for the evening, and so only needed to collect a single keycard. She was as exciting as she was beautiful. Little things like this set his pulse racing like it hadn't for years.

"Room service." calling as he knocked.

****

It was a couple of hours later that the real room service arrived, a couple of hugely overly priced meals and another bottle of eye-wateringly expensive Moet, but Steve didn't care, what was the point in getting all this money if he didn't enjoy it. He enjoyed spending it on his young PA as well.

"I'm going to have a shower." Kissing him as she rose from the bed, and walked gingerly to the bathroom.

As she did, Steve flicked through the satellite TV channels, settling on some generic reruns of old Top Gear episodes. Something inside of him flickered, a sixth sense that he needed to check out. Hearing the water flowing, he knew he would have a fair bit of time, and headed towards the door.

Collecting his black leather bag, and grabbing the phone out of the bottom pocket, he sat back on the bed. A couple of received messages from the unsaved number, he opened them.

We have some concerns. Need you to be more discreet.

Suggest you contact us when you've finished with her.

Steve leaned forward, concern written over his face, and his head began to pound. He grabbed the flute of champagne from the bed side table, inadvertently knocking his wallet onto the floor. Cursing it as it fell. He scrambled over to pick it up, and managed to recover it. Putting the strewn cards back clumsily in their fine leather home, and dumping it alongside him on the bed. Necking the champagne, he laid the empty glass next to it.

Returning to the phone, he read the messages over and over. He still had no clue how they were aware of the events taking place here. They had moved hotel for this sole reason. His content and relaxed moment had disappeared in an instant, his body tense, as he hit reply.

Don't like being spied on.

Instantly, he felt a mixture of anger and regret. Rueing his instincts, he had been fighting so hard with over recent weeks. He should have been calmer, and not fired off a response like that. The phone lit up.

Our deal requires discretion. You are not acting as such. We warned you before. Suggest ending relations immediately.

He took a deep breath this time, intently staring at the message. Why should he stop things with Rachel? The two parts of his life were so separate. Standing from the edge of the bed, he grabbed the flute next to him, walking over to the metal ice bucket. The ice was nearly melted away, but the champagne bottle was cold to the touch. He poured the remains into his glass, drinking it in one mouthful again, and paced towards the window.

Looking out the window, there was nothing but grey buildings and yellow lights. Stevenage was not a city that inspired the mind. In that moment, he wondered if he should make a run for it. Take every penny he had, and disappear. Maybe Rachel would come with him, he mused.

My private life is my concern.

Smooth arms wrapped around his waist. He could feel the heat from them against his dressing gown. She was much shorter than him, but peeked over his shoulder as he locked the phone a split second too late.

"Who is that?" She enquired.

"Nobody, it's nothing"

"I've always wondered why you have another phone, especially where you keep texting numbers you haven't even saved."

"Honestly, it's nothing, just work." He shuffled uncomfortably.

"It's not though is it?" Her tone turning from inquisitive, to accusational.

"Does it matter?" He turned into her, and held her slight frame against his.

"Yeah. It bothers me." She pulled away.

Sitting on the corner of the large bed, staring at him. She had seen him jittery around the phone before, unsure if it was another woman, or his wife. The fact he rarely used the other phone was her biggest giveaway that something was wrong.

"It shouldn't." He tried to shake her off but couldn't. Her gaze focused on his, unwavering.

"If it's another woman, or your wife, then I kind of deserve to know."

"It's just work, I can't explain it."

He paced the room, drifting in and out of eye contact with her. Knowing she was onto something, he felt trapped. Bending over to open the mini bar fridge, he pulled out the small bottle of Johnnie Walker red label, twisting it open, and draining its contents in one movement. Dropping the cap so it bounced off the desk top, shortly followed by the empty plastic bottle, emitting a few drips of liquid as it did.

Rachel just sat there staring, watching him on the edge.

"So it's clearly something serious." Warmly spoken this time.

"It's nothing." Steve resigned, his head low, hands on the desk in front.

"You can talk to me, in case you haven't noticed, I'm pretty good at keeping a secret." Crossing her legs, the dressing gown riding up her pale thigh.

Steve watched in the mirror, like he was watching through a screen, unsure if she was real, could she be trusted? He didn't know.

"No! Rachel! Stop pushing! Fuck!" He stormed, kicking the small metal bin under the desk so it dented and bounced off the wall, rolling limply on the floor. She startled, but didn't move. The heady combination of whiskey and champagne began to cloud his mind, merging with the mists of rage and frustration.

"Who is it Steve? Or I'll leave?"

In that moment, he couldn't let her go. Be it the relationship that was building, his growing feelings towards her, or the fact she knew something wasn't right. The confusion causing his head to spin in the storm, and he sat on the bed, head in hands.

"I don't know." he mumbled.

She shuffled across the bed, the gown pulling further up her thigh, as she rubbed her hand against his back. Steve ignored the sight, preferring to rub his fingers deep into his eyes.

"I don't know," He repeated. "It's hard to explain."

"Try." She rubbed his back, then his thigh.

He pushed her hand away firmly, before leaning forward to open up the mini bar again, searching for another half decent bottle. Rachel edged back, sensing the evening was going downhill, in the back of her mind she considered the danger she might be in.

A second bottle of whiskey was swallowed in the same way as the first. Their remains scattered across the faux ash laminate.

"I think I should go." She picked up her underwear from the floor, and went to stand.

"No!" Steve shouted, grabbing her elbow clumsily, but hard.

"I really need to go." She stared at him, fear rising to the surface.

Immediately he let go, throwing his hands back to his face. Mumbled apologies streaming out of his mouth, a small tear appearing in the corner of his left eye. Rachel sat, the pinkish hand mark on her arm slowly fading, but not completely, into her natural skin colour. She looked at it, then looked at Steve, weighing up her options.

The two sat, Steve's breathing uneven and uncontrolled, streaks of tears down both cheeks. She moved back in to comfort him, which caused him to drop his guard and turn to her.

"I'm sorry. I'm really so sorry, I shouldn't have done that."

"No, you shouldn't." Her voice quaked.

"It's hard to explain." Closing his eyes.

Once he started, he found it hard to stop. Her young, naive eyes glistened in shock, unaware of the impact one man could have on such events. She had never considered such things happened outside of the movies. She moved uncomfortably between comforting him, to straining her mind to follow along.

Like a twisted fairytale, he took her back to where it all began, the chance conversation over a beer in a central London pub. The former boss, giving him a phone number on a piece of card, and offering an enticing investment opportunity. Describing the acres of land he now owned on the beautiful island of Guernsey.

He regaled the early set up details with a similar energy to that which he felt, when he had first heard them. The approach to purchasing reams of share options through unused online trading accounts had blown Steve's mind initially. Clumsily, he attempted to explain the contorted algorithm and advanced coding which enabled the individuals involved to do this at the touch of a few buttons. All of it, designed to mask their moves. Minimise their footprint. Simply, making it look like a large number of small investors got excited over some stock. The burner phones added a necessary layer of security to the deal.

Something so brilliant in its creation. Having just a couple of individuals, in front of a few screens, controlling thousands of automated bots to do their bidding. It was also something which the young woman next to him seemed to grasp rather well. Demonstrating her comprehension to the subject by likening it to fake follower accounts on social media.

His mood dipped again though, once he disclosed the first steps into using the system to invest in his own business. He had seen some decent success, working with snippets of information from around the industry, and feeding it into the mysterious number, but despite the volume of trades they were completing through the huge number of accounts, they were only skimming a few thousand off of each morsel of gossip. At the time, Steve hadn't twigged this was their plan all along, that he was always going to be a pawn in the game.

It was only a few months later that this realisation hit him, he had seen the system in action, and trusted in its ability to hide its originators. They started small at first, a single board level decision communicated out, and utilised to move the stock. That one day alone, Steve made more than a whole year's salary.

Like a drug, he needed more. Taking bigger risks, and putting increased faith in the faceless individuals hiding behind a single phone number. Just with any dangerous addiction, he became desensitised to what he was doing, but justified it in his own mind, as whilst most addicts drained their wallet, this one was filling his.

Shock raced across Rachel's face as he began discussing the destruction of Mark Jeffries, the planting of the email, and the whiskey bottle. She recoiled as he reached out to comfort her, fear now her primary emotion. Scared the man she was falling in love with was able to manipulate, lie, and deceive in such a calm fashion. It was like she was only beginning to see the real man beneath the flash suit, nice watch, and powerful car.

Steve's catharsis didn't stop there, like a Fisherman's spool, it only gathered pace as the end neared. He grabbed both of Rachel's hands to comfort her as he spoke the words he never thought would leave his lips. How he allowed TWG to collapse, to bury Russell, and put himself where they were today. Not for the position, as so many had thought, but money as the only driver. The addictive drive to push the metronomic share price to greater extremes, cashing out, before manufacturing its violent swing in the opposite direction, for greater and greater gains.

Weight eased from his shoulders. Tension leaving the hands which had held hers so tight for the last few moments.

"Sure you really wanted to know?" He forced a laugh.

She had turned distinctly pale, lost for words, and uncertain of how to grasp hold of an emotion to work with.

"But. The money." She eventually uttered.

"All tucked away in a few overseas accounts."

"Dare I ask?"

"Just over seven and a half million."

Her eyes lit up, as much as she tried to hide it, and colour slowly returned to her face. For a young girl growing up without a father, and struggling to get by on a single mother's single salary, money was disproportionately important to her. It was enough to outweigh her fear of the knowledge she had just gained. Her feelings for the man in front of her were shaken, but still standing strong. Slowly, she pulled open her dressing gown.

"Well, I'd hope you can buy me something nice to wear now."

14

Steve flicked the switch on the kettle, a slow limescale-ridden crackle coming from the bottom of the cheap plastic appliance.

"Two sugars?"

"Please." Alison replied.

She had arrived extra early as well, looking to further stake her claim to fill Steve's shoes. Not a murmur from the boss on who would step up, but she felt, deep down, her chances were stronger than the wet behind the ears little up-start Martin Armstrong.

Her experience was far less, she had not been a Director half as long as her junior colleague.

However, the Jeffries incident alone had cemented her loyalty, she had put more on the line in that moment, than anyone else in his clique. That deserved recognising.

"Need some scotch in that?" Came the brash accent from the doorway.

A wince at the question, along with an involuntary eye roll did not go unnoticed by a now shocked Alison Maxwell. She glared at Steve, her eyes demanding to know if this was coincidence.

"Coffee, Phil?" He dodged.

"Ach, why not?" A degree of over confident smarm infused his words.

Reluctantly, Steve grabbed another mug from the loosely hinged cupboard, and spooned in some stale granulated coffee. Bolton had been acting up the last couple of weeks, growing in unwarranted confidence, that was now edging into cockiness territory. This mornings loaded comment was the final straw.

"Wanna wait in my office, Ali? I just need a sec with Phil."

Maxwell was only too glad to exit at this point. Steaming mug in hand, she sided past the Scot, who grimaced like a child about to be told off by the headteacher.

"Phil. Seriously man!" Steve scolded.

"Just messing with ya, boss." the Glaswegian patting him on his thick shoulder as he opened the drawer.

Immediately, Steve slammed it closed before leaning in towards the shorter man. Knocking his hand away harshly.

"Don't you fucking dare pull that shit again!" A hard, firm, but hushed instruction in his ear.

Steve moved past him, purposely brushing his shoulder against his frame so he would move slightly off balance. A slight chuckle caused him to pause in the doorway.

"Got a meeting now, boss," spoon in hand, scraping sugar from the bowl into his mug. "seeing JT about the little vacancy we have."

Unable to respond how he wanted to, Steve carried on silently down the corridor to his office, hearing only the sly chuckle and clinking of a stirring spoon behind him.

"Fucking idiot." He stormed.

"Should I be concerned?" Alison responded.

Attempting to allay her fears, he confessed the details of the set to he had with Bolton at the Christmas party. How he had found the email, and was prepared to cover it up in exchange for keeping his job in the coming months. She took it remarkably well, her savvy mind working a step ahead of him as always.

"Keep him sweet then?" She jested.

"Something like that."

"I guess you know why I really wanted this meeting?"

"Well," Steve looked at the meeting planner pinging up on his phone, "is it not about store fixtures and fittings?"

She chuckled.

"Ali, this isn't easy, you know that." He began.

Her face dropped back to focused concentration on every word coming from her boss's mouth.

"I'm going to bring someone else in for the COO role."

She barely flickered. Calculating how veiled promises had been made to her, but were now not going to be fulfilled.

"Just for a short time, a year, maybe eighteen months." He clarified. "The city is looking for experienced hands right now. I can't put you into that role in those circumstances."

Masking he disappointment, she maintained her expression, hoping Steve hadn't noticed the minute flicker of a facial muscle as he delivered the news.

"He's a great guy. Great experience, you'll get on really well. We need more people tipping the scales against twats like that!" He flung his arm in the direction of the door.

"I understand." she delivered with her best acting skills.

"Now, I haven't spoken to Martin yet, so I need you to keep that secret for now."

Another flinch, another secret to keep.

"After eighteen months, then what?" She enquired, a little harsher than she wanted, so ended with a forced smile.

Steve responded to what he saw, believing she was taking the news remarkably well. She was always going to be the harder of the two to break it to. What he couldn't see was her blood boiling inside.

"Well, then it's down to who's performed best." Challenged Steve, sat back smugly in his large leather chair.

Alison sipped her cooling cup of coffee, holding it in both hands, if only to allow her self a long calming intake of breath, to dispel the anger building in her muscles.

"I won't lie to you Steve, I'm disappointed, after everything we've endured the last few months. I'd thought you'd have the bottle to stand up to the City, and be your own man."

She couldn't resist pushing back at him, she had always challenged and stretched him. Things would seem out of place if she was silent. The bottle jibe was certainly not called for, but it felt good as it sailed, unnoticed, over his head.

"Ali. If you'd been on the board a couple of years then it would be easier. The thing you've got to remember here, is that we are a public company. I've had my knock backs like this, but these things happen."

Steve stood, and came to sit on the corner of his desk, to be nearer to Alison, and more personal.

"Your time will come, you're a great operator. I hope you understand."

Finishing the remains of the coffee, she stood, which in turn caused Steve to stand.

"Thanks, Steve. I appreciate your advice. I need to shoot, as I'm out with Tina today."

With that she departed from the building. For the first time ever, she had lied to Steve.

Morning Martin, pop round when you can. S.

Not minutes after receiving the text message, Martin Armstrong appeared at Steve's door. Knocking politely before entering. The message delivered sharper and colder than to Alison. The younger man was more visibly disappointed, but a short pep talk from Steve had him back grinning in moments.

Martin had never expected the promotion in truth, he would happily continue doing Steve's bidding from one job to the next. Wherever he was required, he would go. The position in the office had been a significant personal challenge. Having to stay away from his wife, and young family, for extended periods during the week. This was causing strain at home, but this is where Steve needed him.

The two shook hands, and Martin departed as cheerfully as he had entered. It felt like a successful morning for Steve, his two closest allies both content in their jobs, and now he was able to add to his team whist keeping the investors happy. This bought his spirits up immeasurably from the distinct low only a couple of days previously.

He and Rachel had departed on great terms. She agreed they would spend some nights apart now, as Steve looked to get back into his more normal husband duties. The last couple of nights they had continued to send flirty texts to each other through the evening, serving the purpose of keeping Steve's adrenaline buzz flowing, but also allowed Rachel to still feel her strong connection to the older man.

Last nights messages, however, had become more intense. As Steve scrolled through them, sat at his desk, he opened those he had not seen yet, sent in the early hours. Until now, he hadn't want her to see they had been read.

Unfurling lengthy messages of admiration and affection, combined with updates on her evening at her local pub. Quickly descending into those describing how much she missed him, and wished they were at the hotel. The last couple becoming less decipherable, clearly she had been going a bit heavier than expected at the Saint Nicholas. Not one for mid-week drinking, she would likely be worse for where when he popped in to see her.

Just as he stepped out, he noticed Bolton at the end of the corridor. Clearly he had just left his meeting with JT and was striding gladly towards him. His phone beeped in his hand.

Got 5? Sooner rather than later if you can. JT x

What had he said in there? He looked too happy to have received the news that the job had already been filled. As he approached, he glanced into Rachel's office before turning and pulling an exaggerated wink at Steve. There were always rumours flying around about PAs in this building, so that could be excused.

"Crikey, Steve," He goaded "No wonder you can't keep your hands off her."

He had always accepted Phil was going to feel this undue sense of confidence, and that it would just need to be managed. However, clearly, now he was edging through arrogance, and into some sort of misguided sense of immortality. Nothing would please him more than taking him into his office and kicking seven shades out of him, but for now, he could only imagine it as he strode by smiling.

"Catch you later, Stevey." A raised hand as he left down the corridor.

Sighing, he popped his head around Rachel's door, just as she was stretching up, mid-yawn, not noticing him at the door.

"Late one?" He smirked, before closing the door behind him.

Startled, her yawn ended as more of a hiccup as her dark ringed eyes fell upon him.

"Oh, er, sorry about all that." Her pale face was now turning a shade of blushing rose.

He placed his big hands on the armrest of her creaky old office chair and kissed her forehead, getting an aroma of alcohol still escaping through her pores. Far more potent than he had expected, it caused him to convulse ever so slightly.

"Wow, big night then!" He recoiled.

"Yeah, a few uni friends were back early for the weekend." She sat sadly back in her seat. Her complexion moving back into the grey/green spectrum.

"Boys?" Steve asked slyly, still leaning over her.

"I don't do boys."

"That's what I like to hear." as he kissed her longingly on the lips.

"When can I see you?" She asked.

"Soon." Steve stood and turned to leave. "I need to lay low for a bit."

"But." She held herself back from spilling her hungover emotions.

He kissed her again, briefly, on the lips, before heading to her door, closing it quietly behind him and turning towards the office of JT. His hand in his pocket spinning his wedding ring around his finger. Sarah had briefly caught on to his increased messaging in the evenings but, for now, he was able to pass it off as work as she sat watching TV.

"Good morning Jane. You called?" He put on his best English for her. More kissing, but this time continental double cheeked style for the glamorous Mrs Tyler.

"Good morning to you too! Full of the joys of spring? Sorry to bother you with this."

"Not at all, go on."

"Phil. He's not winning himself any fans at the moment is he?" A classic JT leading question.

"How do you mean?" Steve feigning his best impression of a shocked Phil Bolton fan.

JT smiled, like a chess player who had been blocked at one of her better attacks. She knew Steve better than that, but never stopped her wanting to play the game a little longer.

"He's just having a grumble." She continued.

"About?"

"FreshCo team, his future, his salary. I sensed he wanted to be asked about the COO role."

Steve couldn't restrain a choked laugh.

"My thoughts exactly." JT smiled.

"Anything we need to worry about?" Steve pushed for more information.

"I don't think so. I think I managed to quash it, but thought you need to know. His attitude is a bit concerning of late."

"I agree." he could tell where this was leading.

"Maybe we need to reconsider the restructure there?"

Steve had been fending off the light jabs about this for a while. Senior members of the board, confidentially, probing about the need for a large IT team. With the FreshCo ground team pulling more than their weight, and at no cost, there was a growing argument for a restructure. To significantly slim down this area, and bump Bolton.

"We still need him a bit longer, Jane."

"So you've said a few times. It would be remiss of me if I didn't push you a bit on that one."

"I appreciate it Jane."

He knew in his heart there was only so long he could fight off the argument. Balancing the risks of an ever more confident and indomitable Bolton, against a questioning board, and investment groups. Taking a deep breath he looked around the room, fixating on the bookcase next to her desk.

"Off the record, what would we save?"

"I can pull something together, on the Q.T. of course."

"OK, but completely under the radar. He can't get wind of it, not in the frame of mind he's in currently."

"Understood, I'll bring Ruth in on it. Totally off book."

"I want nothing to do with it for now." Steve demanded. Clear in his own mind that Bolton was increasingly dangerous either way.

"Ruth is our girl."

With their agreement set, and farewell kisses delivered. The two parted company. Jane would do the job as confidentially as possible, but there was always a risk in it. Ideally, this would have waited a number of weeks, maybe months, until things were more settled. The fact was that the FreshCo guys were running rings around Bolton and his clan, they had taken large chunks of system management up to their Yorkshire base.

Ellie Ash had been instrumental in that, making changes happen at a lightning pace. In turn, she was highlighting Bolton's languid attitude of late. Wherever Steve seemed to turn in the ageing building, she was there. Full of smiles, and laughter, she was clearly building a great rapport with all of the power brokers, everyone except Steve. She rarely engaged him other than in the weekly board meeting, or times when a direct decision was needed.

She had been operating in his blind spot for too long a period now. Sounding out any dissenters in the office, looking for those who would speak ill of him. Some teams had been only too keen to open up to the warm hearted individual. Gathering up her snippets of discontent, all of which were relayed back to her Northern Irish mentor.

15

"Your phone was buzzing all night again." Sarah stormed into the living room.

"Not sure what you want me to say." Steve barely lifted his head from the Sunday financial broadsheet.

"You never used to bring it to bed either." She stood over him, not moving.

He could tell that clear battle lines were being drawn. Whenever Sarah wanted to go a few rounds of verbal sparring with him, she would set herself to the ground like this, especially if he was sat nearby. If he stood, his larger frame would impose on her, and she could play victim.

Folding up his paper dramatically, before tossing it onto the coffee table in front, he turned to face her. A deep sigh left his mouth.

"Do you not think I need to? Sarah, come on."

"No, you work ridiculous hours all week. Why the hell do you need to be on your phone all Saturday? Especially in bed!"

Steve rolled his eyes, something that riled her massively. Their tensions had been building for a while now. He had tried to ignore Rachel's messages numerous times, but her attitude had become increasingly erratic. From moments of relative highs, sending him sexy photos which he had to immediately delete, to desperate pleas for attention. Last night had reached a new low, as she had demanded multiple times for him to leave Sarah and go to her.

"Don't start, Steve, I know it's not work."

"Then what? I'm having an affair?"

"Probably!" She stormed, her hand gestures becoming more erratic.

"Sarah, it's work. Things don't stop anymore. Jesus."

His lie was getting thinner. There was no rational reason why he would be on his phone until the late hours, replying to messages. He knew he needed to stop, but Rachel knew so much. The risk of her turning on him was huge. She could end him in a moment, for now, he needed to keep her relatively sweet, until he could work out a longer term plan.

"It's bollocks Steve." Exasperated, her face reddening.

"I don't need this." He stood, grabbing his paper, and walked around the opposite side of the coffee table.

"Where are you going?" Shock through her voice.

He had not walked out on an argument before. Always preferring to stand and take her on, usually leaving her with tears and presents before bedtime. His patience for it was running thin, but more so, he knew his story was unravelling. The longer he stayed, the more she would find out.

"Coffee." He dismissed with a wave of the rolled paper, and grabbed his coat off the peg, before slamming the front door behind him.

Taking in the fresh spring air, he paced down the street towards the main road. A good walk would help clear his head, and time away from the incessant nagging would be welcome relief. Throwing his jacket over his shoulders, he shoved his hands into the pockets, the wedding ring spinning beginning as soon as he did.

Hitting the end of the road, he turned towards the main part of town.

****

"Mummy, why are you on your phone so much?" Came the little voice from her side.

"Sorry sweetheart, Mummy just has a work thing to sort out." She quickly retracted it into her pocket, and smiled at her husband.

He understood the pressures, and quickly challenged the girls to a race on the small narrow pathway that crossed the open field. The distraction worked, as it always did, as they turned to celebrate beating him for the umpteenth time this weekend.

The short break had been planned in for a while, an opportunity to make use of the beautiful property they had purchased last year. With only a short flight from the UK, it made a long weekend getaway very accessible despite the mounting pressures of her job.

Guernsey had been recommended to her by a former mentor, and now close friend. The very person she was heading into town to meet now, before flying back out later today.

The stroll from the small cottage down to the port took them through winding country lanes, across open fields and eventually down the steep cobbled hill that surrounded it. Only fifteen minutes from their second home, and they were stood on the edge of the beautiful bay, overlooking the expensive private vessels that bobbed up and down in the freezing water.

The sun shined brightly, which gave the whole area a beautiful shimmer. It did, however, present the risk of the dreaded Guernsey fog that was prevalent at this time of year. Something that had the potential to ground flights from the island for days.

Turning away from the bay, the girls laughed happily as they ran up and down the small inclines between the main shopping streets. Unique little shops, with unique crafts, made this feel like they were a world away. She tried to neglect the buzzing of her phone, as the girls dashed in an out of sweet shops and toy stores.

Checking her watch, she kissed her husband on the cheek as he whisked them into the next shop. She slowly strolled down the cobbled street towards the bistro cafe on the corner ahead.

The French influence on the island manifested itself in some wonderful cuisine and various dining experiences. By far and away her favourite, and that of the man now standing to meet her, was Dix Neuf. A quaint little brasserie that hugged the main shopping street. Its blue awned building only very slight in comparison to the large department stores nearby, however, every meal time, patrons would spill out onto the cobblestones, tables spreading further and further every time she visited.

Today, though, an indoor table was required, as they exchanged files, and sat.

****

The cafe was a mellow bustle of clinking china, the double clacks of coffee grinders and wisps of pressurised steam filled the air. Nondescript faces came and went, none of them disturbing the dour fellow sat in the wide leather chair next to the window.

Steve sat, taking a cautious sip of his overly hot coffee, before returning to the large awkward newspaper. He clumsily folded around the article that had piqued his interest back at the house.

Russell's become the latest retail success story.

Now that the partly screwed paper could be held in one hand, he lifted the cheap cup in the other. Able to gently sip the hot brown liquid as he read.

The article had not been a surprise, the communications team at the office had been prepped for it, and able to support its creation. What was a surprise to Steve was the glowing positivity that it contained.

Whilst he had built great relations with the industry level press gang, going national was a whole new ball game. This would do wonders for his reputation, the headhunters would be all over this Monday morning, and could begin opening up doors for him in the coming years.

He had always considered life beyond Russell's, once this phase of his plan had been completed, and he had cashed out his chips.

His phone buzzed, interrupting his thought. Unaware that it had buzzed multiple times on the walk down the hill. Putting his paper down, he opened it to more messages from Rachel.

They were similarly desperate and distraught, as the previous set, but there was a difference here. The timings. All of her messages had been sent this morning, and were comprehendible. She had told him last night that she had been staying in at her Mother's house as she had felt a bit under the weather. He hadn't replied at the time, so was faced with a barrage of accusations of not caring for her.

He continued scrolling.

Clearly you don't give a shit about me. I love you, and this is how I'm treated.

Why aren't you replying again? With her I guess.

Why are you picking her over me? She's a hag.

Steve, I feel awful. Please come and look after me.

I know you love me too.

His phone buzzed as the screen revealed one final message, sent only seconds ago.

You need to call me.

He paused, and looked around, as if expecting one of the few faces sat in opposite corners of this quiet cafe to be watching his moves and reporting back to Sarah. His nerves jangled, as he considered his next move.

Draining the last of the, now warm, coffee from the cup, he pressed call on her number. Rationalising that it would be the only way of putting this to an end.

"Rachel, this needs to stop."

All he could hear was sobbing down the line.

"Rachel, are you OK?" Tension raising the volume of his voice, and grabbing the attention of the elderly couple sat closest.

"No, I need you." She sobbed.

"What's happened? Talk to me here." He began to sense this was beyond the demanding affections of a lovesick personal assistant.

"I need to see you now. Or everyone will know what you've done."

"Rachel." He demanded, again getting the attention of the older couple.

There was now heavy crying on the other end of the line. It sounded like there was nobody with her to comfort her.

"I'm late, and it's all your fault." She eventually pulled together enough.

The depths of Steve's stomach crunched. By now, the old couple were taking in turns to glance at the drama unfolding by the floor to ceiling window of the cafe. Watching the man sat in the big leather chair, phone pressed to his ear as he ran his fingers frantically through his hair.

"Well get a test!" He whispered brashly.

"I've got one, I'm too nervous to do it." She whimpered.

"It's nothing, this can all be sorted quickly." He stammered. "Just do it!"

"I need you here."

"No, Rach. You know I'm not going to do that. Hang on."

Steve stood to leave the small cafe, ignoring the acknowledgement of the young man behind the counter. Tugging the jammed door until it opened, he huffed outside and looked around for a direction to walk.

"I'm not coming." He stood his ground.

"You're a fucking idiot Steve, I wish I didn't love you, I'm crying my eyes out here! And you're going back to that bitch of a wife! You should be here Steve. I could be pregnant! Our baby Steve."

"You're not pregnant." Was the best he could muster, his temperature rising despite the chill air that blew across his face.

"Fuck you, you don't know, you aren't here. Fine. I'll do the fucking test."

****

She stood, and kissed him on both cheeks, before sipping the last of her coffee from the cup. He thanked her warmly for her time, and she reciprocated, before heading back into the now bustling main street.

A broad smile washed across her face as she walked through the street towards the gallery where she planned to be reunited with her family. The information provided to her over the brief coffee would make the week ahead one of the busiest to date, so the opportunity to take in the fresh, clean, island air was savoured.

"Shall we go get our bags then girls?" Crouching to put her arms around them both as they whined.

Her husband stood, large wrapped frame in hand.

"Not sure how Daddy's going to get that home!" She chuckled.

The girls berated their father's choice on the walk back up the winding hill. He had a growing appreciation of art around the home, although this piece would remain on the island. The extra large painting of a family of lions, he reassured Niamh, was a depiction of their own pride.

As they reached the top of the hill, the misty fog could be seen hugging the coastline off to their left side. The last time they had seen it that bad was on one of their first visits to the island, and it had ended up delaying their flight home by twenty four hours. Niamh saw her husband had also spotted the potential issue.

"It'll be fine." He whispered, and put his large comforting arm around her slight waist.

A successful rugby career ended a few years early by a freak ankle injury. However, he still retained his fitness, and with it, his muscular physique. He had transitioned into a wonderful full time father, almost effortlessly. Thriving in his new role, the girls also loved having him around. Especially at the school sports day when their pride in him saw no bounds.

She nestled into his shoulder, and they both watched the girls running the path that cut diagonally across a large field and to the small swing set ahead. Their small shopping bags bouncing wildly in their hands.

****

Steve turned into the local children's park, and sat on the bench around the perimeter. Although there was a brisk chill in the air, there were still two families enjoying the equipment. He sat and watched them as he heard rustled noises down the line. Footsteps approaching in his ear.

"It can take three minutes." She spoke coldly.

Everything moved in slow motion as the children in front of him climbed the fresh new frame, ran across the small wooden bridge and slid down the slide to a cheering parent below. His mind scrambled to grab a cohesive thought to work with.

"It's not happening Rach." He rejected.

"There's a line Steve. I'm pregnant."

"No, that's impossible Rach. I don't believe you."

"I'll take a fucking picture if you want? You seem to like getting them."

Steve stormed away from the park, slamming his feet into the grass as he cut across a corner of the park, heading further away from home. Struggling to comprehend what was real, and how to process it. He hung up the phone.

****

Niamh paced up and down the small run of shops that made up the duty free shopping for Guernsey airport. The girls happily distracted in the world of tablet computing.

She fired off a few emails to her key people warning them of the delayed flight. Currently only a few hours, but the growing risk of this encroaching into her Monday morning routine.

Regular, annoying, updates did nothing to allay her concerns. Snapping a number of times at the family, she had been dispatched to get some retail therapy. Not that she could look at anything right now, she needed to get back. Of all weeks, this was not the one to be stuck here.

Taking deep breathes, she walked over to look at the window.

"The post plane is coming in, that's a good sign." Said the old man next to her.

All of sudden the air around the landing strip appeared to clear, and barely a minute later, lights appeared at one end. The blaring sound of reversing propellers got the attention of all the passengers waiting for good news. The plane turned swiftly into the area by the long window, all eyes on it.

People began gathering bags, and removing headphones, until the true identity of the aircraft was revealed. Bags were unloaded and loaded, before it span back towards the runway and lights disappeared into the sky, flashing in the distance, before being engulfed in white.

"Give it ten minutes." Came the old voice next to her again.

"Ladies and gentlemen, thank you for your patience." Came the crackled, overly loud and cheerful voice, through the tannoy system. "Aurigny airlines flight zero zero three to Jersey, with final destination Manchester, will be landing in approximately ten minutes."

Instructions continued, but fell on deaf ears as clambering and jostling for positions began. They would have only minutes to board, and ensure they could be back up in the air when the fog resumed.

Grabbing all the hand luggage in his large hands, he scooped up their youngest, much to the delight of the pair of fifty something ladies next to him. Niamh shuffled her other daughter towards the door, just as the whirring sound commenced again.

The propellers had barely stopped as they dashed across the tarmac, and climbed the small stair set into the seating area.

Niamh exhaled a huge sigh of relief as the propellers sped up moments later and the small plane lurched towards the run way. As long as the quick turnaround in Jersey went to plan, they would be home before midnight. The girls wouldn't sleep until the early hours, but at least she could be at the helm in the office tomorrow.

Smiling, she nuzzled up next to her daughter at the window as they sped down the dark runway and into the misty sky.

Once airborne, she smiled at her husband who was happily distracting the girls with a game on their handheld console. She delved into her hand luggage, pulling out the file that had been handed to her in the brasserie. Refreshing her mind, one more time of its contents.

****

Tentatively, Steve picked up the phone that had been lighting up every couple of minutes for the last few hours.

"No, Rach, we are not doing this."

"I'll call the doctor tomorrow." Her calm voice down the line, as she stared at the small plastic device in her hand.

"I want nothing to do with this." He spat.

Thoughts span in his head, alongside temptation to throw his phone as far away as possible.

"You are going to have everything to do with this, or everyone is going to know what you've done."

The line went dead.

16

. . . .

"How do you do it?"

"Do what?" A half chuckle as she replied.

"Make it look effortless, nothing seems to knock you."

"I don't know, Steve. I guess I have a good team around me I can trust to get on with it."

"Like Ellie?" He quipped.

"Absolutely, she's a diamond. She's there to help you, you know?" Niamh softly spoken as ever, despite the low rumble of road noise in the background.

He had dialled her number on somewhat of a whim, a sign he was becoming more emotionally driven, less thought through. Events were driving him, rather than the other way around. For now, it was Niamh who was driving.

"I won't lie, I think I need it." He shocked himself with the cry for help.

"We all do, Steve. This shit isn't easy. Nobody teaches you how to be a Chief Executive Officer, whatever the fuck that actually means."

Steve laughed, it felt good to talk to her in this way. They had their differences, and difficult conversations through this process, but she had proved to be a good sounding board, and in time, someone he could trust.

"I'm always here for a chat Steve. Nobody was for me, but given how things are, the line is always open for you."

Listening to he calming Irish drawl, he took a moment to check the phone lying silently at the bottom of the bag, relieved the screen was blank.

"I really do appreciate that, Niamh. You're one of the good ones!" His voice brightening as the call culminated.

"I've got another call coming in Steve, I'll call you back!.

Despite the curtailed call, Steve's chest immediately felt lighter. Necessary for preparing himself for what was coming next.

He stood and left his room, closing the door behind him. As he walked past Rachel's office, he glanced in briefly. Only to be greeted with a dark grey, lifeless room. Normally she would be sat there, eyes gleaming against the computer screen, her golden hair rolling over the back of her chair. He had missed her smile in the last few days.

She had made no contact since the incident on Sunday morning, Steve had needed to make excuses for her absence to those around the building who came asking for her. The silence worried him hugely, she was no longer responding to his texts, or answering his calls.

"Morning, boss!" Came the sunshine voice as he approached the staircase.

"Morning, Colin."

"Baz and I will get all your stuff moved on Friday, is that alright? Anything else we can do for you?"

"No, no, all fine." Steve trying to remain grateful but conscious of where he needed to be two minutes ago.

"Boss, if you don't mind me saying."

Steve had to stop, and smile. As he always had, he needed to keep these guys on his side. A free moving service into the true CEO office couldn't be sniffed at.

"It's been a lot better round here recently since you became boss. Baz and I thought so anyway!"

"Ah! Thanks Colin, and thanks Baz for me as well." He stepped to the side to continue down the stairs.

"I will, always good to see you! Have a great day!"

"You too Colin, cheers again!" he called from nearly the last step.

Only a couple of minutes delayed, he hoped Bolton would still be free. A sneaky check at his meeting planner had showed a free space after a private appointment.

Walking out of the main building, he stopped dead in his tracks and watched. Instinctively, he dropped to untie and then retie his shoe laces, no longer rueing the delay on the stairs.

He watched carefully as Alison and Phil left the IT department together, laughing heavily, before hugging a goodbye. Both Directors then split their separate ways, large grins placed across their faces. Bolton who disappeared around the side of the building, hadn't spotted Steve crouching down. Alison now heading to her car, phone glued to her ear in heavy concentration.

"Morning Ali." he called across the car park.

Her body visibly recoiled at the shout, clearly aware of its origins. She flicked a brief wave with her hand, still holding a large folio bag, forced a smile back, and disappeared into her car. Something was up, but he would need to deal with that later, for now, he needed Bolton, and followed him around the side of the building.

The call to Alison had also caught Bolton's attention. He caught Steve out of the side of his eye and stopped dead in his tracks, before turning and walking back. Confident in his stride and chest puffed, Steve braced himself.

"At your games again, Bellingham?" He stood uncomfortably close.

"I heard you've been making a bit of noise." Sidestepping the question.

"A fucking restructure, Steve." He stepped back to roll an exaggerated laugh.

"I don't know what you're talking about, Phil."

"Bullshit!" His finger pointed, rage in his eyes.

"What do you think you know?"

"Ruth Wickes working on a restructure plan for my fucking department. I thought we had a fucking deal."

He stopped, and laughed, before continuing.

"I should have known better than to trust you. This conversation is over."

He turned to walk away, shaking his head, and muttering loud expletives to himself. Steve galloped to catch up the few paces, and put his hand on

Bolton's shoulder. This caused the man to flinch and turn like he was about to swing a punch.

"Fuck off, Steve. You know what, you're going to get what's coming to you."

The comment froze him to the spot. Watching him leave, the same angry babbling as he reached his car. Steve immediately turned on his heels towards the office, a jittery shake building in his chest and running through his arms and down into his fingers. Clumsily he dialled Alison's number as he walked back into the building.

Straight to voicemail. He tried again, only to be greeted with the same. Another two attempts as he climbed the stairs.

A thought struck him, and caused him to detour. Entering the trading department like a whirlwind, he paced aggressively past the rows of desks. The lack of lights coming from the office to his left telling him what he needed to know.

"Where's Martin?" He called aimlessly.

"He had to nip out, into town apparently." Came the voice beside him. "Anything I can help with?"

He looked at Lucy, her bright, grinning face. Nothing she could do to help. Without response, Steve turned and stormed back to his room. Leaving puzzled looks behind him as the department doors swung closed, as violently as they were opened.

Slamming his office door behind him, he hit the call button once more. Straight to Alison's pre-recorded message yet again. He knew she would be able to see him calling this many times, and was consciously ignoring him. What wasn't so clear was why.

Collapsing into his chair, he tried Martin's number, only to be met by the same connection.

"Fucking hell!" His fist slamming into the desk.

Discarding the phone onto the desk, he stood and moved to the window. Dark grey clouds overhead, rain approaching over the town centre.

His hands raised to his face, running all his fingers through his hair before resting them behind his neck, and closing his eyes.

The first spec of rain hit the window, running down to the sill, and off into the grass below.

****

The door creaked open. A hand reaching knowingly to the metal box on the wall, and pressed the protruding light switch. A low hum, followed by a succession of clicks and dings bought the room into light, and then full brightness as the fluorescent tubes warmed up.

Hard soled shoes paced across the tiled floor, and around the back of the large table. A sealed plastic bag of items hit the surface. At the same time, the fabric office chair squeaked under the weight of its occupant. The bag was now pulled gently open by the large hands, before being tipped out on the makeshift desk. The items scattered loosely, but it was only the plastic case, that clattered as it fell and bounced to a stop, that was needed right now.

A plump finger pulled back its cover to reveal the USB port, and pushed into into the corresponding port on the lifeless computer, bringing additional light into the room.

As the anti-virus scanning complete, the flash drive opened on the screen. A number of documents of varying type appeared in the window. The bulky hand swamping the mouse, moving the arrow over to open the first file, an image flashed up on the screen. The chair creaked louder, as its sitter leaned back.

A sharp exhale of breath, indicating the gravity of what had appeared.

A press of the plastic grey button next to him, bought a crackled buzz, and connection to the outside. He moved closer to the small, stubby, microphone.

"Can you bring them through?"

17

Groggily he unlocked the car door with the remote. He never did sleep well on the spare bed. Whether it was that, or the constant swirling of thoughts, that caused him to toss and turn yet again, all night, he wasn't sure. Last night's half bottle of brandy had certainly not helped this morning's situation.

The blaring of advertisement voices came through the numerous speakers, hurriedly he pressed the preset button for Radio Classic, hoping it would have its usual soothing effect for the drive to the office.

He made his usual half way point detour to the Starbucks drive-thru. Mornings like this always required a little extra caffeine, he thought as he ordered extra shots in his usual large drink. As he sat waiting, he pulled out his phone, noticing a message from Alison Maxwell.

Steve, so sorry. Mum in hospital.

He decided not to reply. He would need to wait even longer for also a decent explanation of her meeting with Bolton. Clearly off the books, private sessions, in both their diaries, days earlier.

He took a light sip of his coffee as he waited at the lights to rejoin the motorway. Chemically, this only added to the anxiety racing through his system. Compounding events, and the lack of sleep.

Drifting across the filter lane, a black Audi narrowly missing his rear bumper. Swerving to avoid him, the driver's hand hammered the horn until he was alongside Steve. Their hand then turned to a single middle finger, shoved in his direction as the car sped off in front.

Angrily he pushed hard down with his right foot, the engine reacted a second later, and his speed built rapidly. The red line on the dial climbing steadily into the triple digits. In seconds he caught the Audi, whose driver clearly recognised him, and brake checked him. Bright red lights filling the cabin of the Jaguar, and caused him to ease off.

Steve turned the wheel, before pummelling the pedal once more, and powering the Jag down the inside. Waving his hand furiously at the driver for having the cheek to flick him off. The acceleration continued past the Audi, until it was just a set of shrinking headlights in the rear view mirror.

Checking his mirror again, he smiled. His foot still touching the base of the footwell. The buzz of speed and confrontation had put a smile back on his face. As he eased off the pedal slightly, a bright white double flash caused him to squint. Returning to the mirror, he caught a slight glimpse of its origin. A newly fitted yellow rectangle on the side of the gantry strut.

The smart motorway lights were off, but he had clearly hit through there over one hundred. Cursing loudly, he palmed the steering wheel causing it to shake. Pulling off onto the a-road that lead towards Stevenage, his anger didn't subside. Any road user that wronged him got the full force of the Jaguar horn. Continuing this pattern right up to the small country road turning taking him up to the office building.

Clambering out of the car, he frustratedly tugged his soft leather bag with him, causing it to catch on the door frame, scuffing the leather with a small tear. He swore loudly, causing the small bird nearby to flurry off into the trees.

"Bad morning, boss?" Came the chirpy voice behind him.

"Like you wouldn't believe." He turned to stare Martin in the eyes.

"Still haven't sorted my phone."

Armstrong scurried for his phone in his pocket, dragging it out and shoving it into Steve's gaze. His fabric laptop bag falling from his shoulder clumsily as he did so.

Steve grabbed the phone, the shattered screen scratching against his thumb. The touch lit up the device, prism like light shining out through the cracks, but no detail could be seen.

Steve handed the phone back between thumb and forefinger, rolling his eyes as he did so.

"Fuck's sake Martin. Get Bolton to just give you a new one."

The younger man stepping quickly to keep pace with the bold, irate, strides of his boss.

"Going to sort it today, boss."

Steve didn't even warrant that with a response, preferring to stew his own thoughts in his mind.

"Need anything else for the FreshCo call?"

"No, we're fine. Catch you later."

With that he stormed down the corridor into his room. The now ritual slamming of the door following swiftly after.

Carelessly he chucked his damaged bag onto the floor, and dangled his suit jacket of the back of the nearest chair before slumping into the one behind his desk.

Niamh's visit would be welcome relief, it would be good to have someone smart around the place, that he could talk to, and was on the same level as him. He checked his watch, rueing that this was still a number of hours away.

Grabbing his phone, he hit reply on the message from Alison.

OK, ring me when you can.

He didn't see the need to be nicer, something still didn't sit well with him. Armstrong's mishap hadn't quashed the growing feeling of distrust towards the two, leaving him with a lonely empty feeling. They had fought alongside him for long enough, he knew them, their moods and their actions. Those of Alison Maxwell yesterday, did not match.

His emotional compass was spinning. Feeling out of control for the first time in years was jarring, and uncomfortable. He sat staring, rubbing his tired grey eyes. Pushing his fingers harder, causing a fuzzy static to shoot through his vision, as if trying to rub out the events of recent days and weeks.

There were too many people who could damage him now. He had been careless, lacked discretion, all rooted in the pursuit of the young vibrant woman, who's life he was now about to ruin.

He had been distracted by her, and it had now taken his eye off the ball in the office. Allowing Bolton to grow in confidence and strength was unacceptable. Only months ago, he would have been dispatched with ruthless efficiency in the same way as Andrews, Russell, and Jeffries. However, he had allowed Rachel to fill his mind, and take up his energy.

To top it off, his drunken revelations to her, in a moment of weakness, he had exposed himself further. The clandestine phone calls were right, he had lacked discretion, and needed to resolve it, fast. His lifestyle, his hidden wealth, all at risk because of a blue line on a pregnancy test. All of it in the hands of a lovesick twenty something.

Raising his head to the sky, he took a deep breath, before reaching into the bottom of his scarred bag for the phone.

Agree. Have been careless. Need help to resolve.

He waited. The responses were normally as swift and effective as their systems. This time there was a delay, minutes passed as Steve kept lighting up the display, waiting for the response. Still nothing. What they would do exactly, he didn't know.

****

Niamh stepped back into her room.

"Sorry gents, urgent family stuff." She smiled, returning the phone to her pocket.

"It's OK, I think we were nearly done now."

The IT experts all nodded at each other as her mind wandered to the implications of the call she had just received.

"Oh, sorry, miles away! Great work guys. I really appreciate the update."

Still standing, she thanked them again, before taking a seat at her desk. She took hold of her large water bottle, flipping open its cap and taking two long sips. Reaching into her bag, she grabbed the flimsy paracetamol packet from the bottom, and popped out two tablets through the foil.

No headache was brewing, but better to be safe than sorry, she thought. One would always come on at times like this, and she needed a clear head. Grabbing her jacket and bag, she paced out to the lift, phone in hand.

****

The ring of his desk phone made him jump. Hurriedly he placed the phone covertly back where it came from and answered.

"Mr Bellingham, can you please come to reception."
The voice nervous, and timid.

Without response, he hung up the line, leaving his jacket and bag where they were strewn, the door left wide open as he headed down the long dark corridor. Something in him span wildly, a tension he had never felt before raged through the muscles in his back. His head light, and spaced out, as he swiped through into the main stairwell, now lit with an oscillating blue light, breaking up the grey morning.

His heartbeat raced as he tried to calmly descend the staircase. Eyes focused on the uniformed police officers waiting at the bottom.

Steph sat at reception, desperate to avoid eye contact with him, as people began gathering over the bannister rail, looking down into the action below. Their excited expressions like children waiting for the funfair to open.

Steve cursed himself. He had never been an angry or aggressive driver, this morning had just got the better of him. Confusion ran through him, as synapses fired in his brain, putting the pieces of the cognitive jigsaw together, and calculating how serious this was. Had he flicked off an undercover policeman? Surely they would have stopped him there and then? Maybe they had reported him? Had he gone through the speed trap over one hundred? Surely none of those would warrant this intrusion into his office. His place of work. His empire.

Confusion subsided, as anger took hold.

"Steve Bellingham?" The older officer addressed him.

"Yes, what is all this about?" Steve dismissed aggressively.

"Mr Bellingham, I am Chief Inspector Wallace, and this is Sergeant Cave. You are being arrested under allegations of share manipulation, and insider trading. You do not have to say anything, but it may harm your defence if you do not mention when questioned something which you later rely on in court. Anything you do say may be given in evidence. If you could please come with us to the vehicle."

Eyes glued on his slumped figure as he was led from the doorway. Word had spread like fire through every room of the building, some still eating and drinking as they watched in hushed confusion.

As his head was guided into the back seat of one of the cars, his heart jolted in his chest. Cold swept through his bones as realisation of what was happening crept in.

Hanging his head low against his knees, tears fell from his face.

18

....

"This morning, we are delighted to be able to talk to Niamh Jones, CEO of FreshCo."

"Thanks for having me guys. Long time listener, first time caller."

Laughter crossed the airwaves.

"Clearly we won't be going into the details surrounding the ongoing case, but it has been two months now, since the arrest of Russell's CEO, Steve Bellingham, I'm sure you're still feeling the shockwaves given your relationship there."

Isobel Dacourt's voice bright and bubbly despite the early hour and topic of conversation.

"Absolutely." She paused, waiting for the killer question.

"Many across the industry have described FreshCo recently, as 'ruthless opportunists'. One article went a bit further, calling you 'vultures'. How do you cope with things like that?"

"Well, first and foremost, you can understand it." She let out a light chuckle, not reciprocated by the two hosts. "it's no real secret that we needed to expand our reach, and be closer to customers, and communities."

The words prepared by her corporate communications officer felt contrite, but necessary.

"Our large stores still have their place, and continue to do exceptionally well for us, but our strategy has always been to push into more of the convenience space. This obviously influenced our work with Russell's originally to supply them through the same network as our large branches."

"Niamh, it's Mikey here. I think we all agreed that was a great move on both parts. Was it working well?"

"Totally, both sides were working exceptionally well together to land it so quickly after TWG went under."

"And then the arrest, seemed to shake the foundations a little."

"Well, as you say, we can't really discuss it, but the business suffered unduly. There are fantastic, loyal, people who work there, and to see them on the precipice of closing hundreds of stores, because of what happened was not something we could sit by and watch."

"But you also had skin in the game." Isobel clarified bluntly.

"Absolutely." Niamh reminding herself to dodge this line of questioning in future. "The fact the systems were in place, and we had the existing relationship with the teams, it was absolutely the right thing for all parties. The leadership team in place there now, know the business so well, and know what's right for it."

"And you got a good deal in the process."

"The financial security provided by the deal will mean that thousands of people will keep their jobs if that's what you mean?"

"Is there any guilt there? The business was about to go under, and FreshCo snap it up at a cheap price?"

"No. Everyone benefitted. If anything, I feel pride."

"I can see why one of those articles called you 'the apex predator of supermarkets' now." Isobel chuckled.

"I preferred 'lioness of the retail industry'. Had a nicer ring to it." Niamh returned. Smiling as she visioned the painting hanging in her holiday home.

"You get portrayed as so tough and uncompromising. Why do you think you get described in that way?"

"Some people just know how to pull strings, some know how to play a system. I think very few can do both with a smile on their face, and whilst looking like they were hardly involved at all."

"What a great answer, thank you so much for coming on to talk to us this morning on Money Matters. The time is seven o'clock, and it's time for the news."

Just as the call ended, the car door closed.

A tap of the jacket pocket confirmed the phone was still safely in there, just as it had been the numerous times it had been checked on the journey up.

Coffee in hand, looking upwards, the view of the large glass building as imposing as ever. Before confidently striding up the concrete steps, and flashing the freshly issued ID badge.

With Steve out of the way, and FreshCo about to plough millions into their newly bought project, things were about to get really exciting. At times, there had been real worries about keeping a job, so being asked to pick up the reigns of the entire business had been somewhat of a shock. Or at least that's how it came across.

The view from the lift to the top floor was stunning. Spring blossoms as pink as the sky, the sun peaking over the horizon. A moment was needed, to let it all soak in, before stepping out, and into the large expansive office.

Doors beeped open as the card pressed against the reader. The route had been travelled many times before, but this was the first time alone. Cursory smiles passed to the individuals on the central desks before heading to the room where Niamh could be seen, tucked behind her desk.

A strong double knock on the glass door, got her attention away from the screen.

"Well that seemed to go really well. They liked you."

The door closed behind, sealing them both in the expansive glass office.

"Morning, you listened? Thanks for that. We needed some good PR, the papers are hammering us at the weekend."

"Well at least the shareholders are happy." Delivered with a broad smile.

"That they are! Try telling the stuffed shirts around here though." Niamh waved her hand towards the other rooms on the floor.

"Am I OK to take a desk out in the middle until my office is ready?"

"Of course, just let me know if you need anything, or anyone gives you hassle."

"Excellent, I'll crack on then."

Smiles exchanged, Niamh's eyes intently back on the screen on her desk, as the office door was opened.

"Oh, Alison. Before you go, I'll take his phone off you. Can't have that getting into the wrong hands can we?"

Printed in Great Britain
by Amazon